PRINCE OF
PERSI
THE SANDS O

W9-AGB-326

TO
RIGHT
A
WRONG

It's YOUR Call
with more than 20 possible endings

Disney **PRINCE OF**
PERSIA
THE SANDS OF TIME

TO
RIGHT
A
WRONG

Written by Carla Jablonski
Based on the screenplay written by Doug Miro & Carlo Bernard
From a screen story by Jordan Mechner and Boaz Yakin
Executive Producers Mike Stenson, Chad Oman, John August, Jordan Mechner,
Patrick McCormick, Eric McLeod
Produced by Jerry Bruckheimer
Directed by Mike Newell

Disney PRESS

New York

In your hands you hold an object of great power. It is an object with the ability to alter the course of history. The choices you make while holding this item will impact moments in time and fateful events, and could even be the difference between life and death for those closest to you.

As Prince Dastan, will you save the beautiful Princess Tamina? Will you try to find your father's killer? These, and countless other choices are yours to make. Will you save the world or destroy it?

It's YOUR call.

Prologue

Before the coming of the Prophet Mohammed, there was a harsh land that few could survive and none could control. But with the bold stroke of a sword and the sheer force of will, an empire rose from its rocky soil. That empire was Persia.

By the close of the sixth century, its reach extended from the beaches of the Mediterranean to the steppes of China. But like any empire, it was only as great as its princes—those who would one day be kings. . . .

Not all princes are born with royal blood. You, Prince Dastan, were found in the streets of Nasaf. You stepped in when one of the king's guards bullied another street urchin, your friend Yusef. King Sharaman admired your honesty, your courage, and your spirit. He saw great potential in you and adopted you into his family. The third and youngest of his sons.

That was twelve years ago. Now your father spends much of his time in prayer and contemplation. And your nation is on the verge of war.

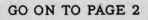 **GO ON TO PAGE 2**

You pace in the war-council tent, just outside the beautiful city of Alamut. Although your father, the king, has clearly stated he wants the city spared, your older brothers—Tus, the heir to the kingdom, and Garsiv, the empire's military leader—along with your uncle Nizam, the king's brother, have decided to attack.

"But our father feels the city is sacred," you argue.

"The king doesn't know about this," Tus says.

"Then why . . . ?" you ask.

"Our finest spy intercepted a caravan leaving Alamut carrying these to our enemies in Koshkhan," Nizam says.

Tus gestures to a spy, standing by two trunks. The man tips them over, spilling weapons onto the ground. Your eyes widen. It's quite a lethal collection. It seems the rumors are true. The holy city of Alamut is not the peaceful place it claims to be. It is a center for making and selling weapons to your empire's enemies.

"We attack at dawn," Tus declares.

You disagree with the decision to fight—your father will be unhappy—but hold your tongue. Tus is in charge here. Still . . . you need to think about this.

Do you obey Tus's orders as a responsible young prince and command the rear battalion? Or do you come up with a plan of your own, possibly averting a bloodbath, but risking failure—and your family's wrath.

If you stick to your brother's plan, GO ON TO PAGE 74.

If you have a different idea, CONTINUE ON TO PAGE 3.

It's now the middle of the night. You can hear the clamoring preparations for an attack on the city's main gate. With a small group of men, you sneak around to the eastern wall, a coil of rope and several grappling hooks slung over your shoulder.

You hear an Alamutian sentry pacing the parapet above you. You'll need to be very quiet. And fast.

You scale the wall as far as you can; then an arrow thunks between the stones above you. But this is no attack—this was planned between you and Bis, your manservant. More arrows pierce the wall, creating a ladder!

You use the arrows to climb the wall. When you're in position, you fling the grappling hook up and over the edge. It lands with a rather loud clunk.

Uh-oh.

The sentry must have heard it. His footsteps come closer. He peers over the side and looks right into your eyes. But before he can sound an alarm, a dagger flies from behind you and slams into him. He topples over the parapet. You send Bis a silent *thank you* as you climb over the wall. Then you drop the long rope to your commandos below.

"Remind me why we've disobeyed your brother's orders?" Bis says, panting as he struggles over the wall.

"Because a head-on attack will be a massacre. I'll need your shield."

"You know, sire," he says, handing it to you, "it appears to me you won't be happy till you get us all killed."

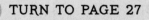 **TURN TO PAGE 27**

4

Everyone freezes. You, holding the Dagger, the guard holding the drawn sword, your brothers, and their men. No one moves. It seems like no one even breathes.

"Prince Tus," Tamina says, "swear to me the people of Alamut will be treated with mercy."

Tus studies her a moment, then reaches out his hand again. This time she takes it. Everyone applauds and cheers. Except you. You find the idea of your brother marrying this princess . . . *unsettling*.

Later, after nightfall, Tus finds you in the courtyard where you have been congratulating your men on their victory. They fall away as Tus approaches, allowing you to speak privately.

"They're calling you the Lion of Persia," Tus says.

You eye him warily. Has he come to admonish you for disobeying him?

"You've never excelled at following orders, Dastan," he goes on.

You grimace. "I have some explaining to do. . . ."

He clamps a hand on your shoulder. "No, we have some celebrating to do." He grins.

You grin back, relieved he's not angry.

"There is, however, a tradition," he says. "Since you took the honor of first assault, you owe me a gift of homage." He eyes the Dagger in your belt and smiles slyly. "A beautiful dagger," he comments.

GO ON TO PAGE 21

As you race down an alley to join the battle, you hear hoof beats. You turn to see a tall man riding an armored stallion. He's heading straight toward you!

You raise your sword, and he draws a scimitar. You're trapped between two walls. How will you get out of this?

You run at the charging horse and at the last possible moment, leap *straight up*. You kick your legs so you can move from wall to wall, then you pull the surprised warrior off the back of his horse. You both land hard on the ground.

He whirls around, slashing at you with the scimitar. You meet him with your sword and the clanging of steel against steel echoes off the walls. He is a graceful, powerful opponent. You use every skill you have to keep him at bay. One of your thrusts cuts an embroidered cloth bundle from the man's belt. It falls to the ground.

You strike again and are surprised that your sword isn't blocked. The man seems to be trying to get to the fallen object. Your blade cuts across the man's flesh, and he drops to his knees. He reaches again for the cloth sack. You knock him out with the hilt of your sword and stand over him.

The sounds of battle rage around you, but you stare at the bundle. What's so important about this pile of cloth that kept the man from defending himself?

If you stop to look inside the bundle,
TURN TO PAGE 122.

If you leave it alone, **TURN TO PAGE 34.**

6

You find your family in the Alamut High Temple.

Stepping inside, you gaze in awe at the splendor of the temple. But nothing compares to the beauty of the young woman being questioned by your uncle and brothers. Her long, dark hair contrasts with her pale, shimmering gown, and the golden chain and amulet she wears around her neck sparkle against her soft skin. Her eyes are dark—and full of pride.

"Princess Tamina, we know you secretly build weapons for enemies of Persia," your uncle Nizam says. "Now show us where."

The woman holds her head high. "We have no secret forges here, and what weapons we have, you overcame."

"Our spies say differently," Garsiv says with a snarl. "Much pain can be spared if you—"

Princess Tamina cuts him off. "All the pain in the world won't help you find something that doesn't exist."

Tus steps forward. "Spoken like one wise enough to consider a political solution." He extends his hand. "Join hands with Persia's future king."

"I'll die first." The princess's lips twist in a sneer.

You tense. She doesn't understand what danger she is in.

"Yes," Tus says softly, but decisively. "Yes, you will." He motions to his bodyguard who draws his sword.

You instinctively pull the Dagger from your belt. Your movement catches Princess Tamina's attention. She looks startled, then cries, "Wait!"

TURN TO PAGE 4

The next day you are back with your men waiting for your father's arrival. To pass the time, you are practicing your wall running.

You race straight at Bis, then leap up and onto the wall to run *above* him. One step, two, then you go sprawling to the ground.

"The third step is the hardest," you say, laughing with the others.

"I didn't see you get to the second," you hear Tus say. You look up to see him on horseback, amused. He dismounts and helps you up.

"We've uncovered signs of tunnels on the eastern edge of the city," he tells you. "I'm on my way there now."

"You'll miss the banquet!" you protest.

"You and Garsiv can handle Father in my absence. You do have a gift to honor him with?"

Your mouth opens, then closes. You shake your head.

Tus chuckles. "I knew you'd forget." He gestures to a servant who hands you a wrapped package. "A prayer robe. A gift the king will appreciate. You fought like a champion for me, Dastan. I'm glad to return the favor."

Tus climbs back onto his horse. Then he imparts one last order. "My marriage to Princess Tamina will assure the loyalty of the people of Alamut. If Father doesn't approve our union, I want you to end her life with your own hand."

You gape at him. He wants you to *kill* her?

TURN TO PAGE 18

8

"I have something for you," you tell your father, handing him your gift. "This prayer robe."

Sharaman smiles, opening the package. He pulls on the robe.

Tus chose well, you think. Your father seems very pleased by the gift.

"What can I grant you in return?" he asks.

You look over your shoulder and nod. Bis and the guard escort Tamina into the great hall.

"This is Princess Tamina," you say. "Tus wishes to make a union with her people through marriage. It is my deepest wish that this win your approval."

Your father stands in respectful greeting. "In all my travels," he says formally, "I've never laid eyes on a more beautiful city, Your Highness."

"You should have seen it before your horde of camel-riding illiterates descended upon it," Princess Tamina says, her voice ringing loudly throughout the hall.

"But thank you for noticing, Your Highness," she adds, no hint of apology or humility in her voice.

Luckily, it seems that your father is more amused than offended. But then his expression changes. His eyes widen in panic. He begins clawing at the prayer robe.

"The robe!" he shouts. "It burns!"

TURN TO PAGE 12

You walk into the banquet hall. Beautiful girls dance, while servants circulate with trays of food. Your father, King Sharaman, sits on a dais, enjoying the party.

Nizam steps up beside you as you gaze upon the opulent, festive scene. "One day, you'll have the pleasure of being brother to a king, Dastan," he tells you. "So long as you remember your most important duty, you'll do well." He gestures to a servant.

"And what's that?" you ask.

"Making sure his wineglass stays full."

You smile at your uncle who grins back. The king raises his hand, silencing the exuberant crowd.

"I'm told another of my sons has joined the rank of great Persian warriors," he declares.

You step forward and kneel before the king. Sharaman gently touches your face.

"We missed you," you tell him.

"I was praying for you and your brothers, Dastan." He looks toward his own brother, your uncle Nizam, then back to you. "The bond between brothers is the sword that defends our empire. I pray that sword remains strong."

TURN TO PAGE 30

Just before dawn you find the person you're looking for—Princess Tamina. You sneak up on her in the desert where she lies sleeping. Aksh paces nearby.

You find the Dagger and take it back. Then you shake her awake roughly.

Tamina scowls. "I take it your uncle didn't listen to you."

You sink down beside her. "Worse than that. I saw his hands had been burned. He said it happened trying to pull the cloak off my father." You shake your head. "My uncle made no move to touch that cloak."

"So the burns . . ." Tamina says.

"He must have been the one who poisoned it. It wasn't Tus. It was Nizam."

"I'm sorry," she says.

"I trusted him. I thought he loved my father. But he didn't."

You stand and begin to pace. "He hated spending his whole life as brother to the king. He wanted the crown for himself." You throw your hands up, exasperated. "But murdering my father. This Dagger. None of it makes him king!"

You turn and face her. You know she has the answers. You're determined this time—she's going to give them to you.

"What *aren't* you telling me?" you demand.

TURN TO PAGE 103

Suddenly there's a commotion at the ostrich pen. A squawking stampede of the gangly birds charges onto the track. The crowd boos and shouts. "You did this!" someone yells. "You tried to fix the race!" another person shouts. People start throwing punches, and Amar's guards rush onto the track to try and catch the rampaging birds.

You notice Tamina by the ostrich pen and smile despite yourself. This was her doing!

Seso and Amar are completely distracted by the chaos. You free yourself and rush to the racetrack, determined to retrieve the Dagger. You leap over the railing, but your foot catches and you tumble to the ground.

You scramble back up, dodging the rampaging ostriches and people trying to catch them. The man bringing the Dagger to be melted struggles to get through the crowd. He holds the Dagger in front of him, using it to protect himself from the fighting.

You grab the man's hand and twist the Dagger from it. With a powerful punch, you knock him out.

"Get to the tunnel!" Tamina shouts.

You race to the tunnel and she meets you there. Together, you charge down the narrow passageway. You can hear Amar and his men in pursuit. But soon the sound of their footsteps recedes, and you and the princess are safely away.

TURN TO PAGE 91

Attendants pull at the robe, but they cannot help. It's been coated with something that melds to the king's flesh. He screams in agony.

Your brother Garsiv shoves past you and rips at the robe. "Aaah!" he shouts. "My fingers!"

"God help us!" Nizam cries. "The robe is poisoned!"

All eyes suddenly fix on you. "The robe Dastan gave him!" Garsiv cries.

You stand frozen, horrified. "Dastan, why?" your father chokes out in a dying breath.

"No!" you cry. You drop down beside him.

"Seize him!" Garsiv shouts. "Seize the murderer!"

"Run, my prince," Bis shouts. "Go!" He pulls you to your feet and shoves you toward the door. Then he lets out a strangled cry.

You turn and see a spear run right through him!

That snaps you out of your shocked state. You draw the Dagger from your belt and stab the guard who killed Bis. He goes down. Another guard heads for you, but he topples over. Tamina has hit him over the head with a vase! You pull her out of the way of a whirling sword and race out onto a balcony. You leap over the side, taking her with you.

Splash! You land in a fountain in the courtyard below.

"I can get us out of here," Tamina says.

You stare at her, wondering why she'd help you.

If you head out on your own,
TURN TO PAGE 127.

Go with her **ON PAGE 13.**

You're just going to have to trust her. "We need a horse," you say.

The princess leads you to the stables, where you mount the great war stallion, Aksh. Tamina climbs up behind you, and soon you are furiously riding away from the city.

It is deep into the night when you finally stop running. You dismount and sit on the bank of a river, staring into it, while Aksh grazes nearby.

You put your hand in the water, then lift it, watching the water fall in glimmering drops. "This stream is a tributary of the river that runs through Nasaf. The water they'll use to wash my father's body."

"You mourn the father you murdered?" Tamina asks.

Your head whips around. "I did *not* murder my father."

Tamina looks deeply into your eyes. "You were ready to risk everything for me."

"I swore to my brother I'd take your life, rather than let any other have you," you tell her.

She leans toward you, her lips almost touching yours. "A dilemma," she says softly.

She moves in, almost as if she's about to kiss you—when suddenly she reaches for the Dagger. You manage to slap her hand away, but she grabs your long sword from Aksh's saddle. She swings it wildly. You leap out of the way—barely.

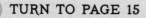 **TURN TO PAGE 15**

"I'm very grateful that you did," you tell Yusef. "But how did you find me?"

"I've followed news of you since that day twelve years ago," Yusef says. "And when I came of age, I joined the army. I was part of your battalion for a while." He takes the flickering torch from the wall sconce lighting the area around you.

"What is this place?" you ask, astonished. "How did you know where the trapdoor was?"

"I have family here in Alamut," Yusef explains. "They taught me about this tunnel. Sandstorms frequently hit, and there are several secret entrances into the city, just in case."

"Ah." You nod. You're glad to be safe from the sandstorm. But if Yusef has family in the city that *your* family has under siege . . .

This could actually be a trap. But he seems genuinely glad to be reunited with you. And he might know where the Alamutians are making and storing their weapons.

If you decide to get away from Yusef and rejoin the battle, **TURN TO PAGE 45.**

If you ask him about weapons, **TURN TO PAGE 33.**

Tamina keeps swinging the sword. You whistle sharply and Aksh turns, slamming her into you. She yanks the Dagger from your belt. You flip her onto her back, sending the Dagger skittering.

Tamina scrambles toward it, but you get there first and snatch it up.

Click! You hit the jewel on the Dagger's glass handle when you grip it. A trickle of sand spills into the air.

The universe warps around you. Time seems to stop. Then it starts to go backward! You watch in awe as images flow past you— reversing themselves.

Your fight with Tamina plays out in front of you, going all the way back to the moment when you thought she was going to kiss you.

You release the jewel and sand stops pouring from the handle. Time moves forward again.

"I have a better solution," Tamina says, just as she did before. She reaches for the Dagger, but this time you grab her arms and hold her tightly.

"Go for that sword again," you hiss, "and I swear I'll break your arm."

"Again?" she repeats. Her eyes widen when she sees the Dagger. "You've used up all the sand!"

You glance at the Dagger. The glass handle is empty. You press the button but this time nothing happens. "What *is* this?" you demand, staring at the Dagger.

TURN TO PAGE 111

You slip the Dagger into your belt. "We wouldn't go to war over one little knife," you scoff. "But if it's this important, I'm sure my uncle Nizam will want to see it."

Princess Tamina scrambles to her feet and throws herself at you, trying to get the Dagger back. "You can't!" she screams. "You don't know the harm you will do!"

You push the princess away hard, and she stumbles backward. You race to your horse and mount, quickly galloping out of the town. Even if she follows, you'll have a head start.

You take the treacherous twists and turns at breakneck speed. You're pretty sure the princess is following you, and you worry that she may have brought reinforcements. Just in case, you pull out the Dagger to have it at the ready should you need to fight.

You take another turn, but your horse stops suddenly, snapping your head back. The Dagger goes flying over the side of a cliff.

You pat the horse's neck. "Good work," you say. You may have lost the Dagger, but the horse's quick reflexes saved your life.

You peer over the edge. There's no way you'll find that dagger now.

That's all right, you think, it probably wasn't very important anyway. The world will go on as it always has. Why wouldn't it?

THE END

"**Y**ou've got to be joking," Tamina says when you tell her your plan. "No one goes near that wasteland. It's filled with murdering cutthroats."

"So they say," you reply. You nudge your horse forward, and it brushes past Tamina.

"You're going to leave me here? In the middle of nowhere?" she demands.

You ignore her and just keep riding.

"Noble Dastan," she calls, her voice dripping with sarcasm. "Abandoning a helpless woman in the wilderness? What does your precious honor say about that?"

You stop and take a deep breath. "Give me the strength not to kill her," you mutter as you wait for her to climb up behind you.

You ride for hours and finally stop. You get down off the horse and scoop up a handful of sand. You refill the handle of the Dagger.

Tamina dismounts and watches you, amused. "Without the right sand, it's just another knife. Not even very sharp."

You press the jewel—nothing happens.

"This sand," you say. "Do you have more of it?"

"Of course not," Tamina says.

You study her, trying to figure out if she's telling the truth. "How can I get some?"

Tamina smirks. "By standing on your head and holding your breath."

TURN TO PAGE 31

"Someday I will be king, Dastan," Tus continues calmly. "When I am, I will need to know you will obey my rule." He studies you a moment. "Can I count on you to do this for me?"

As much as you hate the idea, you nod in agreement.

He leaves, and a short while later you arrive at the princess's chambers.

"I'm to present you to the king, Your Highness," you explain.

She scowls and strides out the door. You have to jog a bit to keep up. Her eyes go to the Dagger in your belt, then back ahead.

"So I'm escorted by Prince Dastan, the Lion of Persia," she says haughtily. "Must feel wonderful winning such acclaim for destroying a peaceful city. Then again, you are a prince of Persia. Senseless and brutal."

You are surprised by her outburst but keep your cool. "A pleasure to meet you, too, Princess. And allow me to offer that if punishing enemies of my king is a crime, it's one I'll gladly repeat."

Tamina snorts. "He's thickheaded as well."

You've had enough. "Don't make the mistake of thinking you know me."

She gives you a snide sideways glance. "Oh? And what more is there?"

A guard stands at the entryway. "Wait here with Her Highness," you instruct him. You turn to face her square on and add, "If you can manage it, I suggest a hint of humility when you're presented to the king. For your own good."

TURN TO PAGE 9

You left the oasis quickly, and now you've been riding at a punishing pace for miles.

"It's safe to stop," Sheikh Amar calls.

You slow down to allow the others to catch up with you. "They won't stop," you say. "They track and kill. That's what they do."

"What *who* does?" Amar demands.

"Those vipers were controlled," you explain as the horses all slow to a walk, "by a dark secret of the empire. Hassansins."

The others stare at you.

"For years, they were the covert killing force of Persian kings," you continue. "But my father ordered them disbanded. Nizam must have disobeyed my father's order and secretly kept the Hassansins intact. We can't stop," you finish urgently.

"Perhaps you can't, but *we* can." Shiekh Amar signals his men to turn around.

"We could use your help getting to the temple," you say. He knows of the quest you and Tamina are on.

Amar laughs. "Not only do you draw trouble like flies to a rotten mango, you're also insane." He starts to turn his horse.

"There's gold at the temple," Tamina blurts out.

Amar stops and looks at her. You can tell he's tempted.

"More than ten horses can carry," she adds. "It'll be yours after you help us. Tax free."

Amar never passes up a deal. He and his men are back on board.

TURN TO PAGE 56

You need to get back to the princess. You say a silent good-bye to your brother, sad that it took such evil to make you both realize the bonds of brotherhood. Slowly, you get back up.

But when you turn, you see Princess Tamina coming toward you. She looks dazed and distraught.

"I'm sorry," she says.

You can't imagine what she would be sorry for. Then it dawns on you. "The Dagger?" you ask.

"It's gone."

She stares down at the ground. "'Protect the Dagger. No matter the consequences.' That was my sacred calling. That was to be my destiny."

She seems so defeated, helpless. This is not the Tamina you have come to know. With the Dagger gone, what is there to do now? You realize with a jolt that the Hassansins' mission was to retrieve the Dagger and return it to Nizam no matter what the cost.

Maybe you should return to Nasaf. Nizam could easily have gone there to install himself as king, and you can't let that happen.

If that's the path you choose, TURN TO PAGE 85.

But what if Nizam has gone to Alamut to pierce the Sandglass of Time? Then you should go there. If that is your plan, TURN TO PAGE 26.

You wish you could keep the Dagger; there's something special about it. But it is less a question and more a demand. You have no choice. Pulling the Dagger from your belt, you hand it to Tus. He holds it up, turning it in the flickering torchlight.

Nizam suddenly appears. "He delivered you the city and its princess," your uncle says to Tus. "I think that's homage enough."

Tus looks at the Dagger, then at you. He gives the Dagger back. "I suppose it is," he says with a shrug.

You shoot your uncle Nizam a grateful look. He smiles back.

"I have wonderful news for you," Nizam says. "Your father has interrupted his prayers at the eastern palace to join us. He'll be here before tomorrow's sun sets."

You hope your father isn't angry that Tus and Garsiv disobeyed him and laid siege to the city. You can tell from Tus's expression that he's worried about the same thing.

TURN TO PAGE 7

You have to get Tus to believe you. "I've seen its power with my own eyes," you tell him. "If we don't stop him *our world could end.*"

He studies your face, considering, struggling to determine the truth. Finally his expression changes and you can see it— Tus *believes* you! At that very moment, Nizam strides into the chamber. "I see Dastan has returned."

He notices the Dagger and a glimmer appears in his eye. Moving quickly, he slashes your brother with a sword.

"Tus!" you cry.

Now Nizam comes after you. You spin, but not quickly enough. He slashes your arm and you drop the Dagger. A gigantic Hassansin picks it up and hands the Dagger to Nizam.

"Oh, Dastan," Nizam sneers. "Always charging in, so desperate to prove you're more than something the king scraped off the street." He strides out of the room.

You lunge for him but are stopped with a swift blow from the Hassansin.

"No!" Tamina screams from the balcony.

The Hassansin whirls around to face her. This gives you your chance. You pull Tus's prayer beads from his hands. You leap up behind the Hassansin and wrap them around his throat. You tug with all your might—until the Hassansin drops to the floor.

"Let's go!" you shout to Tamina. "Nizam's on his way to the Sandglass. I'm sure of it!"

TURN TO PAGE 81

"Uncle, I swear, I didn't murder King Sharaman," you declare once again.

"I'm sure you didn't," Nizam says, still studying the Dagger. He turns and smiles. "But none of that matters now."

"What do you mean?" you ask.

"You'll never know," he declares.

"No!" Tamina shrieks. "Don't do it!"

Nizam lunges forward, catching you off guard. . . .

You blink. Your head feels funny. Then you feel a pain and look down. Your uncle's sword has stabbed you. This is . . .

THE END.

You have to move quickly. Who knows what Nizam is going to do? He could use the Dagger and change the past at any moment. He could also install himself as king before you can make things right.

The moonless night is dark, but you don't care. You'd know the route to the royal compartments with your eyes closed. The inky darkness is a relief to you—it provides the cover you need to make your way through the silent sleeping streets safely.

You hear footsteps and press yourself against a wall. It is only the night sentries making their rounds. They pass without noticing you, and you quickly make your way to a secret entryway—a door you and your brothers used when you wanted to shirk your duties or just get away from the pressures of royal life.

You find the stone that opens the hidden doorway and press it. With a tiny creak, the door pops open an inch. You tug it open all the way and slip inside.

And come face-to-face with three armed guards. All with swords pointed right at you.

TURN TO PAGE 108

You rush out outside the room, looking for Tamina. Without that dagger, there's no way your uncle will believe you.

You spot her rounding a corner. Leaping off a balcony, you take off running.

You quickly catch up with her as she's about to slip into a hidden door that leads into a darkened passageway. You shove your foot into the opening as the door closes. "Not so fast, Princess," you say. "Give it back."

"Never!" Tamina declares. She tries to slam the door shut, but you're too strong.

"Perhaps you'll give it to me." You whirl around to discover you are surrounded by the king's guards. Your uncle Nizam comes toward you. The guards bind your hands.

Tamina turns to run, but the guards are too quick. One fires off an arrow and it pierces her shoulder. She shrieks and stumbles and tries to keep running, but it's no use. A guard drags her out of the passageway.

Nizam takes the Dagger from her. "So this is what all the fuss is about," he comments, holding it up.

TURN TO PAGE 23

You can see Tamina's deep faith has been shaken. Alamut it is.

"We make our own destiny," you tell her. Then, with every ounce of determination you can muster you add, "We'll get the Dagger back."

Sheikh Amar and Seso join you, partners in your plan now. Together, you all head to the Holy City.

When you arrive, you find Alamut is now littered with work sites. Nizam's men are digging, searching for secret armories and forges. Although the men don't know it, you know they're really digging to find the Sandglass of Time.

Tamina hurries over to you after questioning her loyal maidservant. "They've broken through the first level of tunnels," she tells you. "Your brother Tus is still in the city. Nizam is keeping the Dagger in the High Temple." She points to the imposing structure in the middle of the city.

"Then that's where we'll go," you tell her.

TURN TO PAGE 75

You race across the courtyard to open the inner gate while your men work on the outer one. The guards must have heard because suddenly arrows rain down on you.

"Archers!" you shout. "Return fire!"

You reach the inner gate, carrying your own shield and wearing Bis's on your back. This is a critical moment. You get into position and hear a sizzling *whoosh* above you.

You lift your shield as boiling oil pours down on you. It bounces off your upraised shield—then it flows down the shield you're wearing on your back. Your plan worked!

You battle your way to the guard tower. You tip a vat of hot oil onto the street below, then grab a torch from its wall sconce. You fling the torch into the oil, sending up a wall of flame.

You rejoin Bis, and together you push open the outer gate. Your battalion roars into the city.

Dawn is just breaking now. This is when your brothers planned to attack. You've cleared a path for them. You climb onto a parapet to signal your brothers.

The battle begins in earnest.

FIGHT YOUR WAY TO PAGE 5

The sandstorm has not dulled your senses. It would be foolish to follow someone blind while surrounded by enemies. You ignore the person's call and hunker down.

You cover your face with your shirt, to keep from breathing in all that sand. You turn your back to the wind. You can't see a thing, but you try to get to higher ground. Finally you sit and cover your head, hoping the storm will roll over you. You know that some storms last only a few minutes and hope this is one of those.

The roar is deafening and sand pummels you. Quickly you realize it's piling up on top of you. Soon, you can't breathe. You're being buried alive!

Frantically, you try to claw your way out of the sand. But it's no use. This is . . .

THE END.

"What kind of place is this?" Tamina says as you enter the village.

You're wondering the same thing. The structures look more like army barracks than huts or cottages. There's a stable and a locked storehouse. But no people.

"I have a bad feeling . . ." you murmur.

You hear faint chanting. It sounds vaguely like the kind you used to do during your military training.

"What's that?" Tamina asks, pointing to the ground,

Your throat tightens. Furrows have appeared in the ground, as if something is wriggling just below the surface. You've seen this before—and never thought you'd see it again.

"Pit vipers!" you cry.

At that moment, a dozen snake heads burst out of the ground—hissing and flicking their tongues.

TURN TO PAGE 70

You know he's speaking of your earlier disobedience and going against Tus's battle plans. "I understand, Father. I thought my actions would spare our men unnecessary losses."

Sharaman nods. "A good man would have done as you did, Dastan. Acting boldly, courageously to bring a quick victory and spare lives. But a *great* man would have stopped the attack from happening. A *great* man would have stopped what he knew to be wrong. No matter who was ordering it. When I first saw you as a child, those years ago, in that street, I saw a boy capable of being more than just good, but of being great. Tell me, Dastan, was I right to hope for so much?"

You look up and meet his eyes. You can see the deep love behind this challenge. "I wish I could tell you," you say softly.

The king nods. "One day, in your own way, you will."

TURN TO PAGE 8

You scowl and start walking, leading Aksh by the reins.

"You know you even walk like one," Tamina taunts. "Head held high, chest out, long stomping strides. The walk of a self-satisfied Persian prince."

She starts imitating you. You ignore her.

Still she keeps talking. "No doubt it comes from being told the world is yours since birth. And actually believing it."

You can't take it anymore. You whirl around to confront the princess. "I wasn't born in a palace the way you were. I was born in the slums of Nasaf. I fought and clawed to live."

Tamina stares at you, stunned. "Then how . . ."

"The king rode into the market one day and found me. Took me in. Gave me a life. A family. A home." Your fists clench and unclench. "So what you're looking at is the walk of a man who just lost *everything*."

You quickly turn back around and start walking again, not caring if she follows or not.

TURN TO PAGE 89

The soldiers never look up! They race out the other end of the alley, assuming that's where you went.

You drop back down to the ground, wiping sweat from your brow.

Then you do the only thing you can. You head off into the desert. There is someone you need to find.

TURN TO PAGE 10

"We have been told that the Alamutians have secret weapons forges here underground," you tell Yusef. "Have you heard anything of this?"

You watch his reaction carefully. "I have heard the same rumors, Prince," Yusef says, "but I have no direct knowledge of any."

"Could it be true?" you press.

He shrugs. "There are miles of tunnels; I've been in barely a fraction of them. And my family—they are simple people. They wouldn't be privy to such information."

If you could locate the secret forges, you'd be able to bring an end to the fighting quickly.

"What do you say, old friend?" you say, clapping him on the back. "Shall we go hunting for the weapons?"

Yusef grins. "Better than fighting that sandstorm. Or sitting here waiting it out."

You grab a torch from the sconce, and you and Yusef make your way through the narrow tunnel. Very soon you come to a triple fork.

"The one straight ahead leads into the center of the city," Yusef tells you. "The others I've never investigated."

You lift your torch and try to peer down the passageways, but it's no use. The flickering flame just creates jagged shadows.

One tunnel seems to lead deeper into the earth; the other appears to run parallel to the surface. Which way should you go?

If you take the tunnel leading down, **GO TO PAGE 42.**

If you take the level tunnel, **TURN TO PAGE 114.**

You leave the bundle where it is and race out of the alley. Your men need you.

As you dart around a corner, you run right into an Alamutian soldier—and his sword runs right into you.

Gasping, you clutch at the handle, but it's no use. His are the last eyes you ever see. Your brothers will have to fight without you. For you, this battle has come to its bloody . . .

END.

You need to make your uncle understand. "Let me—" you start. Your eyes go to his hands, holding the bundle.

"Your hands, Uncle. They're burned," you comment.

"Yes," Nizam replies. "From trying to pull the poisoned cloak off your father."

Something's not right here. You can feel it.

"Is something wrong, Dastan?" Nizam asks.

You shake your head, stalling.

"You're certain?" Nizam presses. "You know you can trust me, boy."

You look back up into his eyes. He smiles at you.

"Tus is my *brother*," you say. "How could he betray me like this?"

Nizam puts his hand on your shoulder, consolingly. "I can't say, Dastan. Perhaps he never respected you as you deserved. Only saw you as someone he could use."

You frown, recalling Nizam's words at the banquet. "'Someone to keep his wineglass filled,'" you murmur.

Your mind whirls, thoughts colliding with one another. "How many times did Sharaman tell of you saving him from that lion? It was his favorite story."

Nizam's eyes narrow. "One of many."

"No," you press, trying to figure out what is at the tip of your tongue. "That was his favorite."

"I'm afraid you're speaking in riddles," he says.

TURN TO PAGE 83

Despite Tamina's serious tone, you burst out laughing. "I believe in what I can hold in my fist and see with my eyes."

"Then you limit your sight. You miss your sacred calling."

"Spend some time hungry and cold in the gutter," you tell her. "*Then* talk to me about sacred callings."

"I know what the gods have asked of me. And I've dedicated my life to it," Tamina says. She brushes back her long dark hair. "Dastan, I've lost my home, my city—I understand what you feel. But I'm begging you. Stop thinking about what you lost, what you used to be. What are you supposed to *become*?"

You stare down at her, her words slowly sinking in despite your hesitations.

"I suspect it's greater than marching into this funeral and getting your head chopped off," she adds.

You take in a long, slow breath, turning over all the tumult in your mind.

What if she's right? Maybe your destiny *is* to bring the Dagger to the Guardian Temple. But you'd never clear your name, or avenge your father's death. And if she's wrong . . .

Do you do as she asks and travel north to the Guardian Temple? TURN TO PAGE 115.

Do you continue as you planned and enter Avrat to find your uncle? GO TO PAGE 41.

"Hassansins no longer exist," Garsiv hisses at you when you are inside the house.

One of Garsiv's lieutenants bursts in. "Four dead, sir," he reports. "More in the village."

Garsiv nods, but he doesn't lower his blade from your throat.

"Nizam wants me dead," you say. "Wants me silenced. A trial is too public!"

You see something flicker in your brother's eyes. He's starting to believe you, you can tell. "He said as much, didn't he?" you demand.

Garsiv says nothing, but at least he's listening now.

"I know it's never been easy between us," you continue. "But still—you and I are brothers!"

"Touching words with my sword at your throat," Garsiv replies.

"Before our father died he told me 'the bond between brothers is the sword that defends our empire.' He was praying that sword would remain strong."

Garsiv frowns. "Nizam recommended your death," he says. "Tus disagreed and ordered you brought back alive."

"Don't you see? Nizam's using the Hassansins to make sure that never happens. He's afraid of what I might say, who I might tell!"

Garsiv lowers his sword. "Tell me, Dastan."

Thwunk! Thwunk! Thwunk!

Three long metal needles puncture Garsiv's chest!

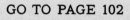 **GO TO PAGE 102**

Later that day, you ride with Sheikh Amar and his men through a desolate rocky valley. "There!" you cry, pointing at a rider in the distance.

The fierce men thunder toward the rider, catching up easily. Now you can see Tamina's furious face. Her eyes blazing, she leaps from Aksh and draws *your* sword from *your* horse's saddle.

But she can't fight Amar's men. One holds her as Shiekh Amar eyes her up and down. He turns to you. "You're right. She's not bad. We have a deal."

Tamina glares at you as you step forward and take the Dagger back from her. You tuck it into your belt. Your head still hurts where she clobbered you.

"Clever princess," you sneer.

GO TO PAGE 67

Still in your costume, you arrive in Avrat, the funeral city of Persia. Just as you had hoped, no one paid any attention to two women traveling together. The disguise worked. But if you have to listen to one more joke at your expense from Tamina, you may use the Dagger to cut out her tongue.

"Do you know where your uncle will be?" Tamina asks. "This is a Persian city, a Persian ceremony. I don't know your ways."

"I've never been here before," you tell her. "But most people seem to be heading in that direction."

You and Tamina blend into the group as you follow the winding stone pathways into the heart of the city. They all seem to be funneling into a compound. "This is where they will prepare the body," you whisper to Tamina. "And where the foreign dignitaries will be entertained." You scan the crowd around you. That's when you realize you are not walking with a group of visiting officials. This is a group of workers.

As you and Tamina step across the threshold, a man stops you. "The women attendants enter the next doorway," he explains.

You gape at him—then you remember your disguise. Clearly it's working!

TURN TO PAGE 64

Y ou do not act too hastily. You need to gather intelligence first. After all, if Nizam isn't here, you'll need to find out where he's gone.

You find your way to one of the poorer sections of the city. You know these streets well. You grew up here until King Sharaman brought you into his family. You still spend time here—carousing with friends, taking part in games and sports.

Tonight you seek Bis's family. Your manservant died on your behalf, and you want to tell his family how brave he was and how proud you were that he was your friend. And you know you can trust them.

You reach the rundown shack and listen at the door. Then you knock softly. It's late, and luckily the streets are deserted. You don't think anyone saw you.

The door creaks open an inch and you see Bis's sister's face. "Yes?" she says. Then her eyes grow wide as she recognizes you.

You shove the door open, grab her, and put your hand over her mouth. You can't risk that she'll give you away. You have no idea where the night sentries might be. You push yourself inside and shut the door behind you.

"I'm sorry," you say, releasing her. "But no one can know I'm here."

"You—you're a murder!" she chokes out.

TURN TO PAGE 125

"Destiny or not," you tell the princess, "if you want to stay close to your precious dagger, you're going to have to help me get into Avrat."

You can see her disappointment and disapproval, but you don't care. You must speak with Nizam and tell him what you know.

Not much later, you and Tamina stand in the crowd lining the streets. You all drop to your knees, and a mournful howl rises. The ornate wagon carrying your father's body is passing. You see Nizam riding at the head of the escort. But you don't see Tus anywhere.

Tus isn't coming, you realize. He's still in Alamut. You don't understand—at first. You grip Tamina's arms, making her look at you squarely in the face. "The sand that fuels the Dagger," you say, "there's more of it hidden somewhere in Alamut, isn't there?"

Tamina's breath catches but then she gives you a tiny nod. You release her.

"That's why Tus stays there. That's what he has our army searching for." Your head whips around to watch the procession pass, Nizam still leading.

You have to get a message to your uncle. You must meet with him and tell him everything. Prove that it was *Tus*, and not you, who wanted your father dead.

TURN TO PAGE 55

"If they're making secret weapons, they'd probably want the security of being on a lower level," you reason. "So let's take this one."

You lead the way down the dark, dank tunnel. Evidence of others who came before you litters the ground. A few bottles, some stray fragments of cloth. Bones.

"Are those . . . ?"

Yusef crouches, bringing his torch closer to the ground. He stands back up. "Just someone's meal. Those are the bones of a pheasant."

You continue on, your heart pounding. Here the tunnel widens, and you see that there are chambers built into the rock face. You notice ancient writings on the walls. "This must have been from an earlier time," you observe.

"There has always been a city here," Yusef confirms, "built upon those that came before."

"But someone ate that pheasant not so long ago," you point out. "So there have been people down here a lot more recently."

Suddenly you signal for Yusef to stop.

There are voices up ahead, around the corner.

TURN TO PAGE 112

Can it be true? Can King Sharaman, the man you called father, who called you son, be so angry because *you* are the one who survived? His adopted son and not those of his blood?

"Perhaps we can make things right," Nizam says. "If we can prove that there are weapons here, your father might see that a siege was the only choice."

"How can we do that?" you ask.

"Convince your father that we must keep digging,"

"You heard him!" you protest. "I don't think I will have much sway with him."

"You underestimate your powers of persuasion," Nizam says. His eyes narrow as he thinks. "There is another way to go. The princess Tamina has vanished. My spies tell me she is hiding somewhere in the city. Find her, and we can get her to reveal the location of the forges."

"Why would she stay?" you ask. "Wouldn't she escape from the city?"

Nizam's eyes flick away. "A woman's motives are hard to fathom."

He knows more than he's saying, but you don't press him. You're far too upset about your father and brothers to worry about some princess's fancies.

"So what will you do?" he asks, looking at you again.

Do you try to convince your father to continue the search for the weapons forges? TURN TO PAGE 126.

Or do you try to find the missing princess?
TURN TO PAGE 72.

Shiek Amar is enjoying your astonishment. "I crafted our lurid reputation to fend off the most insidious evil stalking this forsaken land. *Taxes!*"

You gape at him, trying to figure out if he's serious or not. He is.

"You think these hardworking, albeit slightly smelly desert boys want to win a race only to see their purse halved by some Persian bean pusher?" he says. "No sir! So I came up with a campaign to generate a bit of false notoriety. Now the tax collectors steer clear of me *and* my customers. And everybody's happy."

The ostriches cross the finish line. Half the rowdy crowd cheers and the other half boos. A fight breaks out, and Amar's men swiftly move in to stop it.

Amar shrugs. "Of course, there is the small matter of blood feuds. Ancient hatreds, honor killings . . . They're easily stirred up."

You watch as Amar's guards confiscate weapons and toss them to a slave guarding a locked cage filled with swords, daggers, clubs, and other deadly instruments. These are not men you want to cross.

TURN TO PAGE 98

"I should really get back to my men," you say. "It sounds as if the storm has passed."

"Are you sure you want to risk it?" Yusef asks.

You push up the trapdoor. "See?" you say to him. "All clear." You climb out and find yourself just at the edge of Alamut's city walls. You can hear the horrific sounds of a vicious battle raging—the crash of steel against steel, shrieking horses, war cries, and cries of pain.

You grip your sword. You hope your battalion was able to take cover in the sandstorm, and that your brothers were able to breach Alamut's defenses—all without you.

The gates have been battered open. You quickly charge up the sun-bleached steps, ready to face the fray.

TURN TO PAGE 120

46

"Tamina!" you cry. You rush to her and kneel down beside her. "Tamina, can you hear me?"

She doesn't respond. You turn, thinking you might have something in your saddlebag to help her with when . . . *Thunk!*

You don't know what she hit you with, but it packed a wallop. You fall over as she says, "Yes, Dastan, I can hear you."

That's the last thing you hear. Everything goes black.

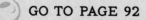 **GO TO PAGE 92**

The sounds of clashing steel and shouts surround you as the Persians and the Hassansins fight. It's total chaos. The air fills with blood, dirt, and cries of pain. You clutch a sword in each hand, lunging and thrusting. You have your eye on the Hassansin with the bandolier.

You fling your sword at him, striking true. He topples over, and you yank off the bandolier. You hurl a grenade and it explodes— just in time to save Sheikh Amar from a halberd-wielding assailant.

You're about to throw another when you turn and discover— Tamina is gone!

"Tamina!" you call frantically.

"Find her," Amar says.

You nod and toss the bandolier to Seso. "Forget the knives, throw these!"

Seso smiles and begins hurling the grenades to create a wall of fire, blocking the Hassansins.

You rush back inside the farmhouse, but she's not there. You hear something moving overhead. You dart back out and pull yourself up onto the roof.

That's when you see it. A crack in the seemingly solid rock face that rims the village.

Yes! You found it! The secret entrance to the Guardian Temple.

GO TO PAGE 124

That's strange, you think. Why would there be sand in a dagger?

Even stranger—images appear around you. The fight you just had with the woman rewinds in front of your eyes.

"I don't believe this," she says. Just as she did a minute ago!

You hold up the Dagger. "This—this turns back time!" you sputter.

"Give that back!" she shrieks. But her injured ankle prevents her from getting to you. You turn and race away. You have to get this Dagger to your father and brothers. This could have a decisive effect on the invasion!

You make your way out of the tunnel and emerge in the city.

And find a complete and utter massacre.

Your brothers are both dead, and there have been many other casualties on both sides. You get word that the terrible toll of the battle caused your father so much despair that his heart failed. He is dead, too.

You gaze down at the Dagger in your hand. You know what you need to do. You press the jewel to turn time back and make a new choice.

And hopefully a new destiny.

TURN TO PAGE 2

The dancing ends and a meal is served. All through the meal your every move is watched. You feel a bit like an animal on display, as if you're being studied. Tamina speaks softly with different members of the group, but you can't understand most of what they're saying. You're relieved when it's time to go to sleep.

You wake up feeling groggy, with a pounding headache. What kind of tea did they give me? you wonder. You try to reach up to rub your face but discover you can't. Your hands and feet are bound. "Tamina!" you cry.

You are soon surrounded by the Shakshi. "Where is Tamina?" you demand. "Untie me!"

The leader comes forward, waving a rattle at you. The others murmur in growing excitement

Now you understand! The princess sold you out! She told them you were a demon and that you were holding her captive.

You struggle to untie yourself as they paint symbols all over you. Soon they are chanting and drumming. Some sort of ritual is taking place, and you are at the center of it.

As the leader of the group stands over you wielding a sharp, two-bladed ceremonial sword, you have the terrible realization of what they have in mind.

You are their perfect human sacrifice.

THE END

The chamber shakes violently, the earthquake reaching full power. The floor cracks under your feet, opening up massive fissures. You leap and clutch one of the columns, hoping it doesn't tumble over.

The walls of the chamber crumble, revealing the sky above. Nizam still struggles to make it to the Sandglass, dodging falling stones and leaping over the cracks spreading through the chamber.

"Stop him!" Tamina cries.

You turn to her and are horrified to see her clinging to a ledge, dangling over a chasm. You have to save her!

"It's not my destiny, it's *yours*!" she screams.

You glance back and see that Nizam has made it to the Sandglass. You watch as he plunges the Dagger into it. *This can't happen!*

You somersault across a widening crack in the ground and land beside Nizam just as he pushes the jewel button. You grab the Dagger, but he clutches your hand as sand begins to flow out of the Sandglass.

Time rewinds around you as you struggle to loosen Nizam's grip.

TURN TO PAGE 131

You need to stay focused on your assailant. You'll find your battalion—and your brothers—once you've dispatched him. Otherwise you might not live to rejoin the troops!

You meet his attack blow-for-blow. You can tell he's tiring. He's losing strength, which is making his aim less accurate. He's growing sloppy.

You thrust your sword again—he deflects it, but you manage to slash him. He drops his sword, clutching his arm, which is now spurting blood. He falls to his knees.

You're about to deliver a deathblow when a cry goes up from the parapets. "The Persians are in retreat! The city is saved!"

You gape at the archers. They're cheering!

This isn't possible!

"We won!" an Alamutian guard shouts. The victory cries now seem to be coming from all parts of the city.

The guard you were fighting grins through his pain. "Not a moment too soon, eh, Persian," he gasps.

You've got to get out of there!

TURN TO PAGE 58

Two days later, your father arrives in Alamut. Nizam has ordered the soldiers to dig up the city in search of weapons. You are still reeling from your loss when he calls for you and Nizam to meet him in the royal apartments of the occupied palace.

"I specifically said I wanted this city spared!" he yells at you and Nizam. "And instead I find a massacre!"

"I tried to tell them—" you begin.

He cuts you off, his eyes blazing with fury. "Do not blame this on your dead brothers," he says. "Only cowards accuse those who cannot defend themselves. And *trying* to do something without succeeding is the same as failure!"

He turns to face Nizam. "I want all digging for the forges to stop. We have destroyed enough of this holy city." He storms out of the room.

You stare down at your feet. You can feel Nizam's eyes on you.

"He was too harsh," he says. "But of course . . ." He trails off.

"Of course what?" you ask.

Nizam looks uncomfortable. "Tus and Garsiv, the sons who died. They were . . ."

"They were his *real* sons," you finish for him. "And I am not." Nizam nods sadly.

TURN TO PAGE 43

"I am Dastan, a prince of Persia," you tell her. "Or I was. Up until a day or so ago."

"How does a prince stop being a prince?" she scoffs.

"When the prince has lost what matters most to him," you reply.

"But you won the battle," she says, her voice hard. "Killing thousands of my people. Persians occupy my city."

You shake your head. "I wanted to avoid the bloodbath the siege became. But my brothers thought otherwise. I lost them in that fight—and my father's favor as well."

"My people lost so much more," Tamina snaps. "And all for nothing! For lies!"

What is she talking about? "We fought your people because you were building weapons and selling them to our enemies!" you declare.

"We have never done such a thing! The weapons don't exist!"

"Why would our spies lie about finding the weapons? Why would my uncle Nizam waste his time searching for forges that aren't there?"

You notice her grip on the Dagger tighten and her eyes flick away.

"What do you know?" you ask.

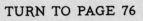 **TURN TO PAGE 76**

Then you hear it—a quiet flutter. You instantly raise the shovel and deflect three spikes. They clatter to the ground.

It's the Hassansin who wounded your brother Garsiv! You let out a war cry and charge at the enemy.

He sends another barrage of needles at you. You leap, twist, and spin under and around the lethal spikes. You hurl the shovel. It ricochets off a column and slams into your assailant.

He stumbles, and you race around him. The Dagger is just inches away.

But then the Hassansin spins and launches another volley. This time you leap straight up, hit the wall with your feet, twist, and push off, slamming feetfirst into his chest.

You pull out your sword and plunge it into the Hassansin. His eyes widen with surprise, then flutter closed. You did it! You defeated him.

Before you have to face another of Nizam's henchmen, you grab the Dagger and leap out the window.

TURN TO PAGE 113

A few long hours later, you stand in an empty livestock room at the edge of the bustling bazaar. Tamina paces outside, standing guard. A man wearing a cloak enters.

"You should not have asked me here, Dastan," your uncle Nizam says, stepping out of the shadows.

While you know it is dangerous, you are grateful that he has come to meet you. You weren't sure he would.

"I didn't kill my father," you state. "You know I would never do such a thing."

"Your actions speak otherwise," Nizam says.

"I had no choice but to flee," you protest. "Tus gave me the cloak. It was poisoned by his hand."

"Dastan—" Nizam begins.

You cut him off. "The invasion of Alamut was a lie. Tus is after power. It's why he murdered the king and framed me for the crime. And now he searches not for forges but for the sand to fuel a mystical device."

Nizam looks incredulous. "This is why you brought me here? Mystical devices?"

"Uncle, do you remember after the battle?" you say earnestly. "You stopped Tus from taking a dagger I'd won."

Nizam nods.

"That dagger is why Tus invaded Alamut. It has incredible powers."

TURN TO PAGE 63

Days later, you arrive at the outskirts of a hidden valley shrouded in mountain mist. Just a few simple stone houses dot the landscape.

You made it!

Amar doesn't look impressed. "I was expecting golden statues and waterfalls," he complains.

Tamina just smiles. "It would be much harder to remain hidden if the riches were so obvious."

You continue into the tiny village. "You're descended from her, aren't you?" you ask Tamina quietly. "The girl that 'won man his reprieve.'"

"Her descendants are Guardians," she replies. "We are trained from childhood to embody the virtue of our ancestors. It's a sacred obligation. Passed down by blood, through generations."

You study her, trying to understand the weight she must carry on her shoulders.

"Your real parents," she says. "What do you know of them?"

You don't even have to think about this one. "Sharaman was my real parent." You swallow, not sure if you want to tell her this, but somehow . . . "Before he died, he asked me if I would be more than a good man. If I'd be a great man."

"He sensed your calling," she says.

You hold the Dagger out to her. "Don't cut yourself, Princess,"

Tamina smiles and takes it. You feel better returning the Dagger to the one who is meant to guard it.

TURN TO PAGE 118

At the very last moment, you swerve and vault a table full of goods, landing in the middle of the merchants. As everyone screams around you, you upend one of the tables, spilling colorful cloth onto the ground. You use the table as a shield and—*thunk!*—a crossbow arrow pierces it. You scurry through the square, knocking over tables, hurling anything you can into the path of the soldiers. You whirl around a corner into an alley.

Thundering footsteps can be heard from behind you. You pant heavily. You're never going to outrun them.

You take a deep breath and leap up. You press your hands and feet against the opposite walls of the alley, suspended above the road. You don't know how long you'll be able to hold your position. Sweat beads up on your forehead.

"This way!" Soldiers charge into the alley.

TURN TO PAGE 32

You spin around to race back out of the gates. But you run right into a group of Alamutian warriors escorting Persian captives to the work camps.

You are quickly bound and added to the group of prisoners.

There will be no escape. You will spend the rest of your days doing hard labor for your enemies.

THE END

After a long, hard ride across the vast desert, Tamina points to a stunning island of lush green and sparkling blue—an oasis. "Our journey is blessed," she says.

You stop and lead Aksh to a rippling pool of water. Clumps of tall grasses and wildflowers wave in the breeze. As Aksh drinks, you and Tamina fill your canteens. Something rustles in the brush. An ostrich steps out, its bulging eyes blinking. You blink back.

You whirl around to grab your sword, but it's too late. A man stands in front of you, tough and heavily armed men emerging from the bush behind him. You recognize this man. It is Sheikh Amar. You've had run-ins with him in the past—and they did not end well.

"We parted under such rushed circumstances," Amar says smoothly. "I never got to say good-bye."

His men circle you, and the biggest, Seso, quickly takes your sword—and the Dagger.

"We've been tracking you for days," Amar adds.

You notice something odd. Sand funnels dance and whirl on top of a nearby dune.

Amar glances in the direction of your gaze. "Sand dervishes, Persian," he says dismissively. "Common as camels in this desert."

"Sheikh Amar, listen to me," you begin.

"I'd rather not." Amar signals his men and they seize you. They gag and bind you. In a moment, Tamina's gagged, too.

TURN TO PAGE 119

Just when you think your luck has run out . . .

"Ogav!" Yusef calls out, stepping in front of you. "What is this place?"

Ogav looks startled. "Yusef! What are you doing down here?"

"We were caught in the sandstorm and were looking for a way out," Yusef explains. He turns to you. "Ogav is one of my cousins. And this is—"

You cut him off. "I'm Shazar," you say. "A friend of Yusef's."

Yusef looks at you quizzically. Yusef may trust Ogav, but as the prince of an invading empire, you don't want to take any chances.

The two other men rise, their expressions grim. Yusef doesn't seem to notice the tension. He steps deeper into the chamber. "Where are we?" he asks.

Ogav's eyes flick to the two other men. Then he shrugs. "It's an ancient treasury. Holding a fortune."

Ogav circles behind you and Yusef. "Up until now," he says, "we were pretty sure we were the only ones who knew about it."

You don't like the feeling of his breath on the back of your neck.

"We want to keep it that way," Ogav snarls.

Do you take out Ogav, and hope you and Yusef can then handle the other two? TURN TO PAGE 62.

Or do you try to talk your way out of there?
TURN TO PAGE 61.

"Any cousins of Yusef's are friends of mine," you say, slowly backing away. "And I keep my friends' secrets. If you don't want anyone else to know about this treasury, they won't know about it from me."

You fling your torch at the men as you spin. "Run!" you shout.

You and Yusef race away as footsteps pound loudly behind you. Up ahead there's another fork. "We should split up," you tell him. "Make it harder for them."

"Good plan," Yusef says, panting.

Yusef veers left while you take the tunnel on the right. A moment later you hear the footsteps once again behind you. It sounds as if none of them followed Yusef.

At least he'll be safe, you think.

You're running blind—this stretch of tunnel has no torches. You stumble but regain your balance, then you slam right into the tunnel wall as it forks again. The wind is knocked out of you. As you catch your breath, you peer around one of the corners. Up ahead is a lone flickering torch.

Should you grab it? It would be a lot easier to navigate if you could see!

But the light will alert Ogav and his pals to your location.

Do you take the torch? TURN TO PAGE 129.

Or do you leave it where it is and keep running in the dark? TURN TO PAGE 71.

You act quickly. With a sharp jab of your elbow to his windpipe, Ogav drops to his knees. "Weapons! Yusef!" you shout. You draw your sword. Yusef draws his.

But instead of facing the two other men, he's looking straight at you.

"But Yusef—" you begin.

"So sorry, Prince," he says. "I know I owe you a debt. But you know the old saying about blood being thicker than water."

"You mean gold is thicker than loyalty," you retort.

Yusef shrugs.

Your leg shoots out in a powerful roundhouse kick, knocking the sword out of Yusef's hand. You leap and kick again, this time at his head. He lands hard on the ground, out cold.

The two other men face you, and you're thrilled to see neither is armed!

Then one bends down and picks up a strange-looking device—something you've never seen before.

The man pulls the trigger, and dozens of barbed pellets shoot out. You scream in pain. Now the other man flings a curved blade at you. You collapse to the ground, landing beside Yusef, mortally wounded.

All those years ago, maybe you should have made a different choice in regard to Yusef. And a different choice today. If you had, this wouldn't be your . . .

END.

"This dagger," Nizam says slowly, "you have it with you?"

This is it. This is your chance to clear your name and make Nizam understand Tus's treachery.

You pull up the sleeve of your cloak, revealing a bundle strapped to your forearm. You untie it and hand it to your uncle. He slowly unwraps it. A puzzled expression comes over his face. He holds up a silver nutcracker.

"Is this some sort of joke, Dastan?" Nizam asks you.

You grab the bundle. The Dagger is gone. It was replaced by a nutcracker so you wouldn't know it was missing. But how . . . ? Who . . . ?

Princess Tamina! You look out the door and discover she's gone. Of course.

Your uncle stands there, waiting. Bewilderment slowly turning to anger on his craggy face.

"I had it, Uncle—I swear."

"Then where is your so-called evidence?" Nizam demands.

Do you rush after Tamina to get the evidence you need?
GO TO PAGE 25.

Or do you continue to plead your case?
TURN TO PAGE 35.

You and Tamina are sent to work in the bathhouse, where foreign representatives go to refresh themselves after their long journeys.

The fat, cranky, red-faced woman who is in charge of the baths studies you and Tamina. "The gentlemen prefer attractive attendants," she says. She frowns at you. "You'll need to stay behind the scenes. You can fetch the heated water. You," she says to Tamina, "you'll be a greeter."

You nod, afraid your voice will give you away. When she leaves, you grab Tamina's wrist. "This is our chance," you whisper. "You must get a message to Nizam." You gaze down at your ridiculous dress. "And I must get some more appropriate clothing!"

You quickly sneak through the area where the visitors change—and steal a new set of men's clothes.

This feels a lot better, you think, as you tuck the Dagger into your belt.

Tamina comes by carrying a nutcracker and a bowl of walnuts. She rolls her eyes. "They are very demanding in there," she says. Then she does a double take. "Dastan! You're . . . *you* again!" She gives you a look you cannot read. A mixture of hate—and curiosity?

You give her a courtly bow. Then you grow serious. "What about the message?"

She nods. "It will be delivered within an hour."

GO TO PAGE 55

It seems you are going to dress like a girl. You duck behind a bush and remove your clothing. Tamina does the same. You throw your clothes to each other.

You feel ridiculous. What made her think this would work? You split the fabric across the back, since your shoulders are a lot broader than hers. And it only comes to just below your knees, since you're also a lot taller.

"Don't laugh," you call as you prepare to step out.

"No promises!" Tamina shouts back.

You come around your bush as she emerges from behind hers. You stare at her. She has somehow fashioned your trousers and shirt into a remarkable garment, and she looks more beautiful than ever.

"It's a good thing you're not trying to find a husband," she says with a smirk. "No man would have you."

"Just do something so that this disguise will work," you say.

She gives you her cloak to hide the tears in your dress. Then she rips some fabric from the hem of the trousers she's wearing and fashions a veil. "Can't have your beard give you away," Tamina says.

She steps back and eyes you critically. "Hmm. Something's not quite right," she says. She reaches out and begins to tug and pat you.

"Not so fast," you say, grabbing her wrist. "You're not getting the Dagger."

Her face hardens for a moment, then she says, "Can't blame a girl for trying."

TURN TO PAGE 39

A few people dressed in strange clothing appear. Then a powerful looking man steps into the chamber. Suddenly, the rewind stops.

"Who are you?" he demands.

"I am Dastan, Prince of Persia."

The young man smirks. "Then you are my prisoner. I am General Alexander, and I have annexed Persia for Greece."

You gape at him. You remember him from your history lessons. This man before you is none other than Alexander the Great. You have gone all the way back in time to around 330 BC!

You're not thrilled to be a prisoner, but you are quite excited to see what life was like a thousand years ago. And maybe, just maybe, you'll figure out a way to get back to your own time . . . eventually.

THE END

Amar and his men bring you and Tamina through a tunnel. Even though her hands are tied, you wish they'd gag her as well. Tamina's been insulting you nonstop.

You hear a commotion up ahead. This is where you and the princess are going to part ways. You bargained with Amar to spare you by promising the princess would work for him.

"Give me a moment with her?" you ask Amar. The sheikh nods, and you pull Tamina to the side. You rip the amulet from around her throat. You open it and, just as you suspected, find grains of glowing sand inside.

"Dastan, listen to me," Tamina says.

You pour the sand into the Dagger, then slide it back into your belt. "When my uncle sees the power of this Dagger, he'll believe our invasion was a lie. Thank you, Your Highness."

"Dastan, that Dagger is sacred," Tamina implores you. "It's only allowed to leave Alamut if the city falls. It was being smuggled to safety when you stole it. If it falls into the wrong hands . . ."

"Don't worry, I'll keep your knife safe," you say.

"You don't understand what's at stake! This is a matter for the gods, not men."

"*Your* gods," you tell her. "Not mine." You turn away from her and nod to Amar. His men drag her away.

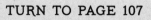

TURN TO PAGE 107

"No one will believe I'm a girl," you protest. "It will be a dead giveaway that we're in disguise."

Tamina eyes you. "You *would* make a pretty ugly woman," she says.

You point to the caravan heading your way. "I'm sure those travelers would love to trade their clothing for my armor. And your fancy garments."

The caravan approaches. It's a strange, motley group. Both the men and the women have kohl-rimmed eyes and are covered in tattoos. Their somber clothing is embroidered with symbols you've never seen before.

"Shakshi," Tamina murmurs.

"What?" you ask.

"I've seen members of this sect before. They believe they are in touch with the darker forces. They travel from town to town offering to rid citizens of evil spirits."

"Do you believe that nonsense?" you ask her.

Tamina shrugs. "I believe in forces beyond mortal understanding. And I have certainly seen evil."

"Are they dangerous?"

"Only if you're a demon," Tamina says. "Let me do the talking," she adds. "They speak an unusual dialect."

She calls out something in a language you don't know. A tall, skeletal man steps out of the group. He must be the leader.

TURN TO PAGE 104

You tie your shirt around your nose and mouth to keep out the sand, duck your head, and follow the voice into the unknown.

"This way!" the voice calls again. You can barely hear him over the howling wind. But you sense you are not too far behind. Suddenly you stumble over him as he kneels at a trapdoor.

You help him tug open the door and quickly jump down after your rescuer. He slams the door shut above you.

It's suddenly quiet. The storm still rages outside, but underground you can hear the stranger's every breath.

You tear the shirt from your face, wanting to see who it is that saved you. A young man about your age looks back at you, grinning.

"I owe you my life," you say.

"Just returning the favor," the young man says.

Now you're puzzled. "Who are you?"

The man bursts out laughing. "You don't recognize me! Well, we have both changed a great deal since our days in the streets. I'm Yusef!"

You smile and pull him into an embrace, clapping him on the back.

"We're all grown up, aren't we?" you say, laughing.

"If you hadn't saved me from the king's guards all those years ago," Yusef says, "I might never have made it to adulthood!"

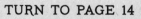

TURN TO PAGE 14

Aksh whinnies and shies, rearing in panic. Tamina lets out a shriek as she falls off, landing hard on the ground.

Instantly, the vipers surround her.

You gain control of Aksh, spinning him around. You draw your sword and lean out as you charge toward Tamina. You slice off the head of one of the vipers just as it's about to strike her. This gets the attention of the others.

Now they come after you.

You slash one viper after another, but you know there's no way you'll be able to get them all. Then you realize Tamina is hurling boulders at them, smashing the ones behind you. And your horse stomps them, too. Finally the last one is dead.

You dismount to make sure Princess Tamina is all right and that your horse wasn't bitten. They both seem fine.

"We have to get away from here as quickly as possible," you say.

"You've seen such creatures before?" Tamina asks.

"They are the tools of the Hassansins," you explain. "A secret, elite group of killers. My father disbanded them. Clearly they are back in business."

The skin on the back of your neck prickles. You're being watched.

TURN TO PAGE 121

You don't want anything to give away your position. You turn down the dark passageway and leave the torch where it is.

Wham! You slam into something—or rather, some*one*! A woman, by the sound of the surprised shriek.

"Are you all right?" you ask.

"Who are you?" the voice in the dark says. From the position of the voice you can tell you knocked her to the ground.

You feel around in the dark, and manage to help her up. She gasps. "My ankle!"

Ahead is a lit passageway. "Let's get to where we can see," you say. "I can bind your ankle."

"I don't believe this," the woman mutters.

You reach the twist in the tunnel where torches line the walls. You see that the woman you crashed into is quite beautiful. As she gazes at you her expression changes from one of discomfort due to her injury to pure fury. Suddenly she pulls out a dagger. "Get away from me, Persian!" she shouts.

You realize she's an Alamutian—and not very happy about the fact that your army has her city under siege.

She lunges at you, but you deftly sidestep her thrust. You whirl around and kick the Dagger out of her hand. You scoop it up. She flings herself at you, making your grip slip. Your fingers hit a small jewel embedded in the Dagger's handle. Sand trickles out of the weapon.

TURN TO PAGE 48

72

"I don't think I'll have any luck with my father," you say sadly. "I'll search for the princess as you suggest. She may provide information that will make our case."

"Good." Nizam nods approvingly.

But how will you find her? Then it hits you. Her servants may know, and may also be willing to reveal the information—for the right price.

You get to the servants' quarters and find several women gathered around a dark-haired beauty.

"Get out, Persian," the beauty snaps. "This is not a place for you."

"And clearly you don't know your place," you admonish her. The other women glare at you. Nevertheless, they shush her.

"I have a few questions . . . and an offer," you say. "I'm looking for your mistress, the princess Tamina. And I will pay handsomely should the information be correct."

The feisty one crosses her arms over her chest. "What makes you think any of us would commit such a betrayal?"

You take a closer look at her. You notice an intricately carved dagger in the waistband of her skirt.

She's not a typical serving girl. Not at all.

"Nice to meet you, Princess Tamina," you say.

TURN TO PAGE 90

You enter the village and discover a beautiful young woman at the fountain. She's filling a bucket. She's startled when she sees you.

"What brings you here, stranger?" she asks warily.

You dismount and approach her. "Chance," you tell her. "I gave my horse the lead, and this is where he brought me. I don't wish to disturb you, but I have been traveling for days. My horse and I could use water, food, and a place to sleep."

She frowns, studying you.

You pull a leather pouch from around your neck. "I can pay."

"Princess Tamina," an elderly woman calls from the doorway of a hut. "The stew is ready."

Your eyes widen in shock. Standing right in front of you is the woman your uncle thought held the key to the secret weapons forges. The woman he wanted you to find.

She takes a step back, her hand suddenly going to an ornate, ancient-looking dagger in her waistband. A weapon you hadn't noticed until now.

Should you take her prisoner, and bring her back to Alamut? **TURN TO PAGE 80.**

Do you pretend you don't realize who she is? What would be the point? **TURN TO PAGE 110.**

At dawn, you are near the southern end of the walled city. Per Tus's orders, you will lead your commandos as backup for your brothers as they breach the main gates.

You wait anxiously for the signal. A wind is whipping up, and the horses are beginning to grow jumpy. You walk the ranks, giving encouragement.

Then you hear a sound you know and fear—the deep howl of a sandstorm. You turn to discover a dark wall of sand heading toward you.

There's nowhere to take cover! You can't wait for the command, you have to get inside the walled city. "Charge!" you shout as you race to get back to your horse, holding your sword high.

But it's too late. The sandstorm is upon you.

The horses whinny in fear and you sense confusion among the men. The sand pounds you, disorienting you, blinding you.

You have to find shelter, but this is unfamiliar terrain. You don't know which way to turn.

Suddenly, a voice says, "This way, Prince. I can get you to safety."

Do you follow the unseen stranger?
TURN TO PAGE 69.

If you think it's too risky, **TURN TO PAGE 28.**

Soon you are approaching the High Temple, wearing the work clothes Tamina's maidservant stole for you. Tamina, too, is dressed in worker's garments. Sheikh Amar and Seso have made themselves scarce.

"I'll meet you in the courtyard," you tell her. "And then I'll bring the Dagger to Tus and prove my innocence."

She gazes at you, her eyes full of concern. You know what she's thinking: you'll only meet her *if* you survive.

You hold up your shovel to cover your face and walk past the guards. Then you follow the directions Tamina gave you to the sanctuary.

You step inside and walk past the ornate stone columns, every sense on alert. It's eerily quiet. Blades of sunlight slash the cool temple darkness. As your eyes adjust, you see the Dagger sitting atop a pedestal, illuminated by a shaft of light.

But no sign of a guard, Hassansin, viper—nothing.

This can't be right, you think.

TURN TO PAGE 54

You see her considering, trying to decide what to tell you.

"The truth, Princess," you say, tapping her with the point of your sword.

Suddenly she flings her bucket at you, knocking you in the forehead. Tamina leaps away and races across the village square.

You rush after her and lunge, hitting her at the knees. She falls with a cry, and you leap on top of her. You quickly wrestle the Dagger away from her. You hold it to her throat. "I've lost my patience. I will come back here and raze this village if I think you're telling me lies."

You feel the fight drain out of her. Protecting the village must truly matter to her.

"That dagger you hold," she says. "Treat it with respect."

You continue to sit on her as you examine the Dagger. "It's pretty. Nice jewel on the handle. But it's just another weapon. Why should I respect it?"

"That's where you're wrong, Persian. This is not just another weapon. It is for this dagger that lies have been told—false excuses to invade our city, to dig beneath our streets. And it is my destiny to protect it."

You stand and step away from her. You can tell she's telling the truth. The truth *she* believes. You just don't buy it.

TURN TO PAGE 16

King Sharaman turns the Dagger over in his hands, examining it. Then he hands it back to the princess. "Yours is a holy city. I will not desecrate it further by claiming your sacred relics."

Princess Tamina clutches the Dagger, her eyes wide with surprise. "Thank you. Perhaps I am wrong in my assumptions about the Persians."

"We have much to learn about each other," King Sharaman says. "Let me suggest an alliance between our peoples. And to seal it, I would like you to marry my beloved son, Prince Dastan."

Now it's your turn to stare. "But I thought . . ." Could Nizam have been wrong?

He gives you a kindly smile. "Even a loving father must sometimes speak harshly to a son."

Princess Tamina looks disdainfully at you, but then nods. "I agree. I am grateful for the respect you have shown my people and our beliefs. I can only hope your son shares your wisdom."

King Sharaman laughs. "We all hope for that!"

You gaze at the princess. You're not sure why, but somehow you feel marrying this arrogant, willful, and beautiful woman is part of a larger destiny. If nothing else, she has given you back the knowledge of your father's love, and for that you are grateful.

THE END

You climb up onto Aksh and gaze down at Tamina. She stares up at you, her eyes wide.

"You're going to help me?" she asks, incredulous.

You feel something shift inside you, something momentous. This is no longer about proving you didn't kill your father. This is about something much bigger. More important. Maybe that "destiny" she spoke of . . .

You hold your hand out to her. "We can sit here and chat," you tell her, grinning, "or you can get on the horse."

TURN TO PAGE 59

You quickly seek out Tus. While Tamina hides on the balcony outside your brother's chamber, you step inside. "Hello, brother," you say quietly.

Tus spins around. "Dastan!" He must have been praying—he's holding your father's prayer beads.

Tus's bodyguards instantly rush toward you. You lunge for Tus and grab him. You hold the Dagger to his throat. The guards freeze where they're standing.

"We need to talk, brother," you say.

"Then talk," Tus replies.

"Alone," you say.

Tus pauses a moment. "Wait outside," he tells the guards.

Once they leave, you look into Tus's eyes. "Alamut was never supplying weapons to our enemies," you tell him. "It was all a lie. Fabricated by our uncle Nizam."

"Nizam?" Tus repeats incredulously. "Are you mad? What could he gain from such a thing?"

"Beneath the streets of this city is an ancient force. A container holding the fabled Sands of Time. Nizam wants to use it to corrupt history and turn back time to make himself king."

Tus is not buying your story. "If you're going to kill me, best you do it now," he says.

TURN TO PAGE 22

You immediately draw your sword. "Pull that Dagger and I will cut off your hand," you tell Princess Tamina.

"Who are you?" she demands. "Why have you come here?"

"Destiny, I suppose," you tell her.

She startles at your statement. "What do you mean?"

You laugh. "Destiny is a far more impressive word than luck," you say. "I was asked to search for you, and I refused. Yet I find you anyway. Doesn't that sound like destiny to you?"

"Why were you looking for me?" she asks. Then her eyes narrow in anger. "You're one of the invading Persians. One of the crude and illiterate buffoons who desecrated the sacred city of Alamut."

"If you care so much for your city, why did you run away?" you retort.

Her jaw sets. "I had my reasons. None that *you* could understand."

"Try me," you say.

"Who are you?" she asks again. "You still haven't told me,"

You waver. What will get you the information you need?

If you decide to tell her the truth, **TURN TO PAGE 53.**

If you decide to lie, **TURN TO PAGE 101.**

You will have to mourn Tus's death later. Now you follow Tamina down a dark staircase. You hope you can stop Nizam in time. "The Guardians built passageways underneath the city for secret access to the Sandglass," she explains.

Tamina finds a carving on the wall and reaches behind it. A hidden door instantly springs open. "If we move fast enough, we might get there before Nizam," she says, echoing your thoughts.

You follow Tamina, coming to a narrow bridge. As you cross it, there's an angry rumble. Pieces of rock crash down around you, falling away into the deep chasm.

"The digging is undermining the city!" you say.

"It's the gods," Tamina cries. "Nizam must have breached the Chamber of the Gods!"

You get across the bridge and emerge from the tunnel. You stand before a vast room with a floor of golden sand. This is the home of the Sandglass of Time.

TURN TO PAGE 94

Both choices are risky, but you'd rather take your chances with the main roads. The Valley of the Slaves is notorious—and you have enough trouble as it is.

"We'll need some sort of disguises," you tell Princess Tamina. "We're both much too recognizable."

"We're not exactly traveling with extensive wardrobes," she points out. "All I can think to do is to dress you in my clothes."

You gape at her. "Dress like a girl? And what will *you* wear?"

She shrugs. "I'll think of something."

You notice a caravan off in the distance. Many travelers come here on their way to market. Maybe you can trade with them for some clothing—perhaps even travel with them, helping you disguise your identity even more and offering you some protection.

On the other hand, no one will be out looking for two young women traveling together.

Tamina is waiting. Which is it going to be?

Swap clothing with her and TURN TO PAGE 65.

Wait for the caravan and TURN TO PAGE 68.

You start to pace, connecting your thoughts. Through a window you notice an archer up on a nearby roof. He wasn't there before.

It wasn't *Tus* behind all this. It was *Nizam*! He never tried to take the robe off Sharaman. His hands should not have been burned.

You take off running.

Vwip! An arrow grazes your side, but you don't stop.

"Dastan!" your uncle calls behind you. "Wait! I can speak to Tus!"

You don't slow down. You race through the crowded marketplace.

You hear footsteps behind you and see crossbowmen on the roofs above you. A two-tiered assault! Another arrow comes at you. You drop to your knees and slide, feeling the arrow's breeze as it whistles by. It clatters to the ground beside you.

You leap up and start running again. Now you see a squad of soldiers coming toward you! Your eyes flick left, then right. Nowhere to go.

You rush straight at them.

 GO TO PAGE 57

You're wasting your time fighting this one guard. You have to find your brothers—and your battalion.

You put all your weight behind your next blow, and the Alamutian topples over. You spin around and race away, your eyes scanning for your Persian comrades.

As you sneak through the city, you are greeted by horrific sights. Carnage is all around you—bloody evidence that the battle has been a massacre. While you were fighting the sandstorm and hiding in the tunnels, Persians and Alamutians were losing their lives in great numbers.

This was precisely what you'd hoped to avoid. It is why you came up with an alternative plan. Maybe if you had gone with your gut, all this could have been avoided.

Then you see Roham, one of your men. He seems dazed, but unharmed.

"Prince Dastan," he calls when he sees you, "I've been searching all over for you."

"What is the news?" you ask as you hurry to him.

The look on his face makes you wonder if perhaps you don't want him to tell you.

TURN TO PAGE 109

"I have to stop Nizam," you say. "I'm all that stands between him and the crown, and he's made certain that I appear guilty of my father's death."

You can't bear to look at the disappointment and defeat on Tamina's face. Maybe once you confront Nizam you can find the Dagger for her.

You say your good-byes to Tamina, Amar, and Seso. Then you mount Aksh, all the turmoil weighing heavily upon you. You have no idea what you're going to do once you get back to Nasaf.

It's a long, hard ride. Your thoughts are no clearer as you approach the city walls. With every mile you've traveled, the more your anger has taken over. When you arrive, you learn Tus is dead. No doubt the result of Nizam, you think. Your anger deepens.

You know where your uncle will be: in the royal compound. It would be easy to sneak in and confront him with such knowledge. It's the middle of the night—perhaps the element of surprise will allow you to get the best of him. Maybe even find the Dagger.

But maybe it would be better to wait and gather information. Nizam might not even still be in the city. You'll need to find a place to hide. After your childhood in the streets, that shouldn't be too hard.

If you confront him now, TURN TO PAGE 24.

If you find a place to hide out and wait, TURN TO PAGE 40.

You drag the princess to Nizam. "Princess Tamina," your uncle says, "so nice of you to join us."

The princess fumes silently beside you.

"Tell me, Dastan," Nizam says, getting up and crossing to stand in front of her. "Did she have some kind of . . . weapon on her?"

You're surprised that he seems to know about the Dagger. You glance at Tamina.

"So the true motive is revealed," she sneers.

You stare down at the Dagger. "You mean it was all for this? But why?"

"Yes, Nizam, why?" King Sharaman enters the room. "You're not the only one who has spies in his service. I understand you told Dastan that I was sorry he was the son who had survived. Why would you tell him such a cruel lie?"

You gape at your father, then at Nizam. You turn to Princess Tamina. "What is so special about this Dagger that my uncle would lie, betray his family bonds, go to war?"

"The Dagger has properties that make it powerful. So powerful," Tamina says, her eyes gleaming, "that I have dedicated my life to protecting it!"

In a swift move she snatches back the Dagger. She dashes onto the balcony and leaps over it.

"Leave her be," King Sharaman says, glaring at your uncle. "We have a far greater enemy here in this room. Guards!"

Tamina may have gotten away, and you may never know the mystery of the Dagger, but you are grateful for what she did reveal: the truth about your uncle—and your loving father.

THE END

You spin, ready to make your escape. *Thunk!* Suddenly you can't move!

A knife has ripped through your cloak and pinned you to a wooden post. Seso, the large, bald African you encountered earlier, stands grinning beside the sheikh.

"Trading her for a camel in Herat?" Shiekh Amar scoffs. "Look at the girl—she's worth at least two!" He circles you. "And you, my friend—your brother Tus has offered a reward for you that, between the two of us, borders on the obscene. I'd turn in my own mother to collect *that* much gold."

Seso gives Amar a disapproving look.

"What? You didn't know what she was like," Amar protests. Then his voice grows serious. "Take him to the Persian outpost."

You notice Tamina hovering near the ostrich pen. She seems to be enjoying your predicament.

Seso reaches to remove the knife that has you pinned. His eyes rest on the Dagger in your belt. "Nice knife," he intones.

You reach for the Dagger, but Seso grabs it first. He hands it to Amar, who gives it an admiring glance. He tosses it to one of his men down on the track.

"Melt it down for the jewels," Amar orders.

TURN TO PAGE 11

Everyone stares at you. Nizam's eyes blaze with fury. He lifts a hand to signal to a bodyguard. "Remove the criminal," he says.

Before the bodyguard can get to you, a tri-bladed knife slices his hand. His sword clatters to the ground.

Your eyes widen in shock. Seso has saved you!

Guards rush toward you, as another grabs Nizam and pulls him off the platform. Now Sheikh Amar appears and blocks their path with his well-armed men.

This is your chance. You rush toward Nizam, but the guards head straight for you. Suddenly the canopy over the platform collapses! It drops down and covers the guards. You're stunned to see Princess Tamina standing by one of the poles, grinning. *She* did this!

"We couldn't let you do this alone," she calls.

Turning, you fling yourself at your uncle, knocking him over. Quickly you grab the sacred Dagger from his belt.

You raise it high over your head. "This is what King Sharaman died for!"

"Don't believe this ungrateful wretch!" Nizam shouts. "King Sharaman took him in off the streets. Dastan never lost his criminal street ways."

The crowd murmurs. You can tell they don't know who to believe.

TURN TO PAGE 116

Soon you come upon a disturbing sight. A sun-bleached skeleton mounted on a stake. Wind rattles through its eye sockets. More skeleton sentries stand behind it.

Tamina gasps. "Who were these people?"

You gaze upon the bones. "Years ago, this valley held the biggest salt mine in the empire. Until the slaves rose up and killed their masters." You nod toward the skeletons. "I heard they boiled them alive."

You glance at Tamina. She just nods, looking pale.

"Welcome to the Valley of the Slaves, Your Highness." You grin.

As you lead Aksh into the valley, Tamina trails behind. "I'm desperate for a drop of water," she complains.

"That's more than we have," you say, "since you emptied our canteen hours ago."

"I wasn't born of this desert like you Persians," Tamina says. "My constitution is more *delicate*."

"I think you mean *spoiled*," you reply.

"The wells of Alamut are famous for their clean, cold water," she says.

"Perhaps if you spent less time admiring your wells and more guarding your walls, you wouldn't be here," you quip. When she doesn't respond to your dig you say, "A miracle! I've silenced the princess."

You turn to gloat but instead see that Tamina has collapsed on the sand.

TURN TO PAGE 46

Princess Tamina's women surround you as she tries to run. They attempt to stop you, but you're too quick. You grab the princess and yank the Dagger out of her waistband. The women throw themselves at you, kicking, biting, scratching. You grip the princess's long, dark hair, yank back her head and bring the Dagger to her throat.

"One more move," you warn her servants, "and she dies."

The women fall back. Princess Tamina betrays no fear, just fury.

"You have no right to touch that Dagger," she snarls. "You're not worthy!"

"Well, then I guess someone who is worthy will have to escort it." You carefully release your hold on her hair, but still clutch her arm.

"Escort it where?" Tamina demands. "What do you plan to do?"

Good question.

Should you bring her to Nizam? Perhaps he can question her about the forges and get vital intelligence. GO TO PAGE 86.

Or should you bring her straight to King Sharaman and try to make peace with your father? GO TO PAGE 97.

The next morning, you and Tamina ride Aksh at the end of a long trail of people heading to your father's funeral. You have continued your journey safely away from the Valley of the Slaves. Now you approach the imposing gates that lead into Avrat, the funeral city of the Persian empire.

"There's got to be a hundred Persian soldiers watching those gates," Tamina says, worried.

"Maybe more," you comment.

"Please," Tamina implores you. "We must take the Dagger north. There's a Guardian Temple hidden in the mountains outside Alamut. Only the priests know of it. It's the one place the Dagger can rest safely."

You don't respond, you just keep walking.

Tamina clutches your arm. "Why do you think your father took you off the street that day?"

You turn and gaze at her, wondering why she asked that question. "I suppose he felt something for me."

"Love?" Tamina asks. "He very well may have." Now her expression grows more thoughtful. "But that's not what was at work. It was something far greater. The gods have a plan for you. A *destiny!*"

TURN TO PAGE 36

Your head throbs as you lie flat on your back on the ground. You sense movement around you. You slowly open your eyes—and see a dozen men on horseback surrounding you. They are armed to the teeth, dressed in a battle-worn mixture of Persian finery and Bedu cloaks. These must be the slaves from which the valley gets its name.

You're about to leap up when—*thunk!*—something lands between your legs. A tri-bladed throwing knife. You stare at the still-quivering ivory handle. One more inch and . . . you don't want to think about it.

"Do you know where you are, Persian?" a turbaned, powerful looking man demands.

Your eyes leave the weapon and travel to the man's craggy face. You nod.

"And yet you enter?" the man asks.

You nod again.

"I am Sheikh Amar," he says. "This is Seso," He points to one of the riders, a tall, bald, African man, wearing a bandolier of tri-bladed knives across his chest. He is spinning another in his hand.

"Tell me, Persian who enters our valley uninvited," Amar says, "is there any reason I shouldn't ask Seso to put his next throw just a bit higher?"

You gulp, and frantically try to think of a story to get yourself out of this predicament.

TURN TO PAGE 38

Tamina suddenly jumps up and pushes past you.

"What are you doing?" You grab her by the arms, stopping her.

"There's only one way to stop all this," she says. "To be sure the Dagger is safe."

"How?" you ask.

"The first thing we learn, if all else fails," she says. "Put the Dagger back in the stone. The Dagger will disappear forever, returning to the gods."

Before you can ask more questions, you hear the sound of hoofbeats and the clanking of weapons. The Persian cavalry bursts through the trees.

There's nowhere to run, no way to escape. You're surrounded.

Then your brother Garsiv dismounts and strides toward you.

"Garsiv," you say, "listen to me. There are four dead priests over there. Murdered by the Hassansins. On Nizam's order. *He's* the traitor!"

Garsiv laughs, sending a chill through you. He draws his sword and holds it to your neck. Then he pulls you inside a small farmhouse.

TURN TO PAGE 37

94

The gigantic Sandglass seems to have grown from the rock itself. It holds thousands of tons of glowing white sand that bathe the chamber in an ethereal light. You and Tamina hover in the shadows. Nizam has arrived ahead of you.

There is another deep rumbling. You rush to stand between Nizam and the Sandglass. You pull out your sword. "You murdered your own family!" you cry, your voice echoing in the vast chamber.

Nizam grips the sacred Dagger. "At first I thought it would be difficult," he says. "But in the end it wasn't. Just like any war."

"Sharaman was your brother!" Your voice is nearly drowned out by the cracking sounds around you.

"And my *curse*," he spits back.

A piece of the ceiling clatters to the ground. An earthquake is rattling around you.

"How could you have done this?" you demand.

"Do you know what it's like, boy?" Nizam says, now beginning to circle you. "No matter what lands you conquer, what glory you bring the empire, when you walk into a room all eyes are on the man next to you. And you know, if only on that day so long ago, you had simply let him *die* . . . it would have been *you*."

TURN TO PAGE 130

The Hassansin sweeps the sword at your legs. You leap up and tumble over the edge of the roof. You crash to the ground, the wind knocked out of you.

Before you can get back up, the Hassansin lands beside you. His hand clamps around your throat. You struggle against him, clawing at his hands. You can feel the life being choked out of you. Your eyelids begin to flutter.

Suddenly the Hassansin loosens his grip and tumbles over.

You shove him off you and jump up, gasping for air. You are shocked to see a sword has pierced the Hassansin's back.

"Dastan . . ." a voice calls.

You turn to see your brother Garsiv, the needles still protruding from his body. He used his last ounce of strength to save you. That's *his* sword in your assailant.

You rush over and kneel beside him. "Garsiv!" you cry. You can see the light in his eyes fading.

"The sword is strong, brother," he whispers. "Save the empire."

You grip his hand and watch as the life drains out of him. He's gone.

TURN TO PAGE 20

"Long ago," Tamina says softly, "the gods looked down at man and saw nothing but greed and treachery. So they sent a great sandstorm to destroy all, wipe clean the face of the earth. But one young girl survived."

She pauses as if she's not certain she should keep going. You nod at her to continue.

"She begged the gods to give mankind another chance, offering her life in exchange. The gods looked down on her and, seeing the purity within, were reminded of man's potential for good. So they returned man to earth and swept the sands into the Sandglass.

"As long as the sand runs through it, time moves forward and man's survival is assured. The Sandglass controls time itself. It reminds us our lives are in the gods' hands. That we are mortal."

TURN TO PAGE 105

You drag Princess Tamina to where your father's chambers are now located.

"I see you wasted no time making yourself at home," she says bitterly. "As if we had never been here at all."

"That's what happens to our enemies," you tell her. "You should have thought twice before making weapons to use against us."

You push her in front of the guard. "I have Princess Tamina here. I want her to speak to King Sharaman."

The guard announces you, and you step inside the chambers. You gaze at the man you called father. It is hard to accept Nizam's theory—that he never cared for you the way he cared for his true sons.

"Father, I have found Princess Tamina. I am sure she will confirm our spies' information about the forges. You will see my brothers did not die in vain."

"I confirm nothing," Tamina declares. "These are all lies."

King Sharaman studies her. "Why would our spies lie to us?" She shrugs.

You sigh. She is truly stubborn. You decide to speak up. "This seems to be very important to her." You give your father the Dagger.

"And *what* is this, princess?" he asks.

Her jaw clenches. She seems to be making a decision. "It is a ceremonial object. Some—perhaps those insisting on digging up our city—ascribe it certain . . . powers. But to Alamutians, it is simply sacred."

TURN TO PAGE 77

"I believe our deal is going to work out quite well," Sheikh Amar says, drawing your attention away from the weapons.

You turn and see that the sheikh is watching Tamina. She's now wearing a skimpy, not very clean outfit and carrying a tray of fermented goat milk, which she is serving to the crowd. She does not look happy. One of the rowdy customers tries to grab her and she smacks his hand away.

"Full of life," the sheikh says. "Where did you find her?"

You quickly try to think of a good cover story. "In the slave markets of Lur," you reply. "I was bringing her to Herat to trade for a camel when she attacked me."

Sheikh Amar nods. "Camels are safer."

"Noble Sheikh Amar," you say respectfully, "I appreciate your hospitality, but if you can give me the supplies we agreed on. . . ."

Amar nods, smiling. But his smile changes, and there's a new glint in his eyes. "It's odd, Persian," he says. "You bear remarkable likeness to the disgraced prince who fled after murdering the king."

Your heart leaps. He knows!

TURN TO PAGE 87

It is dawn the next morning. You tear your blanket into strips and wrap them around Aksh's hooves.

"What are you doing?" Tamina asks.

"Garsiv can't be far behind us," you reply. "Aksh is the most famous horse in the empire. We need to obscure his tracks."

"Tracks where? Where are you going?"

"The holy city of Avrat," you say, swinging up onto the horse. "Where Persian kings are buried. My uncle Nizam will be there for my father's funeral. He's the only one I can trust. He'll listen to me—see I was set up by Tus."

Tamina steps in front of the horse. "You're wanted for the king's murder. And you're going to march into his funeral, alongside thousands of Persian soldiers?"

"Step aside, Princess."

"Every road to Avrat will be covered with Persian troops," she points out.

She's right. You've thought about this all night. You figure you have two options—go in disguise and take your chances on the main route, or avoid the roads and go through the Valley of the Slaves.

If you decide to chance it on the main roads,
GO TO PAGE 82.

If you go through the Valley of the Slaves, **GO TO PAGE 17.**

You can't risk using the Dagger. If you run out of sand, you are not sure what will happen.

Instead, you use the Dagger to slash the lead viper's head off. Seso leaps to his feet and grabs one of his tri-bladed knives. He hurls it at another viper, but the evil creature ducks and coils again. In a flash, it strikes Seso, who collapses as the venom quickly works its way through his system.

The commotion wakes Sheikh Amar and Tamina—just in time for each of them to be bitten by the deadly snakes.

Now those snakes turn to you.

That's it, you think, I've got to use the Dagger!

But just as you slide your hand down to hit the jewel, a viper lunges. It sinks its teeth into your hand. You cry in agony and drop the Dagger. You fall to your knees clutching your hand.

Now all three vipers hiss as they circle the Dagger. Their tongues flick and dart. They grow blurry to you. The venom is doing its work. You collapse to the ground. This fight has come to its . . .

END.

"My name is Trila," you say. "A mere soldier."

"You say you were charged with finding me," Tamina sneers. "But you refused. You are clearly a man without honor."

"You will be the prize that restores that honor," you tell her. A movement catches your eye. You instinctively fling one of your small knives. An elderly man drops to the ground.

"You *barbarian*!" Tamina shrieks. "That man is a holy man! A Guardian of the Temple! And you killed him for no reason!" She pulls the Dagger from her waistband.

"Don't do it, Princess," you warn her. You bring your blade to her throat.

She laughs sharply. "Typical. You think violence is the only way."

You watch, puzzled, as she makes no move to strike you. She simply holds up the Dagger and presses a jewel on the hilt. Sand trickles out of the handle. You feel fuzzy. How strange! What kind of weapon has sand in it?

Your head clears—just as you hear Tamina say, "Typical." Then you feel a sharp pain in your chest. Looking down, your realize you've been shot by an arrow. You will never clear your name or see your father again. This is . . .

THE END.

Horrified, you stare as Garsiv drops to his knees.

"Garsiv!" you cry. You glance out the doorway and see the mist begin to swirl and twist, forming funnels.

Hassansins!

You rush outside to where the Persian soldiers are still guarding Tamina, Amar, Seso, and Amar's men, unaware of the grave danger they are in. "They're going to attack!" you shout.

You grab Tamina's hand; she grips the Dagger with the other.

Black stallions burst out of the funnels of mists and thunder toward you. Spurring their massive steeds, the Hassansins' voices rise in a horrifying war cry. They draw their weapons, and your stomach clenches. You've never seen such a lethal assortment!

One swings a two-headed ax known as a halberd; another lashes the air with a bladed whip. One wears a bandolier filled with fire grenades. And then there's a giant man wielding a scimitar that looks large enough to block the sun.

"Stay behind me," you order Tamina. To the others you shout, "We have to protect the Dagger!"

The battle begins!

TURN TO PAGE 47

Tamina looks worried, but then you realize it isn't because of what you've been saying. You turn to see what has her transfixed. A sandstorm is heading your way!

"We've got to move," she says.

You hold up the Dagger. "If you want the Dagger back, tell me everything. No more lies."

She nods. "But first can we get out of here?"

"Only a princess would think she can outrun a sandstorm." You guide your horse to sit on the ground, then use the saddle blanket and a sword to create a tent. You and Tamina huddle together inside.

"What secret lies beneath your city?" you ask. There must be something that Nizam believes will help him take the crown, you think.

Tamina is quiet for a moment, considering. Then she says, "In Alamut rests the beating heart of all life on earth. The Sandglass of the Gods."

Outside the wind howls.

TURN TO PAGE 96

As the man and Tamina speak, you are able to recognize a few of the words the princess uses: clothing, journey, trade. But the rest is indecipherable. Then you hear something surprising: demon.

The group all looks at you. "Did you say I was a demon?" you demand.

"Of course not." She points at two children heading toward you holding armfuls of clothing. "Just giving them reasons to trade."

The caravan sets up for the night. You follow the boy and Tamina follows the girl into the lean-tos the nomads have quickly put into place. When you emerge, you see your armor being handed around and Tamina's elegant gown draped around an old woman's shoulders. You tuck the Dagger safely into your cloak.

Tamina appears wearing the dark skirts and cloak of the Shakshi.

As several men make a fire, the rest of the group chants, draws symbols in the sand, and makes odd gestures in the air.

"They have rituals for everything," Tamina explains.

Then they do something even stranger—they bury your armor!

"That's valuable stuff," you exclaim. "If they don't want it, I'll take it back."

The Shakshi stare at you. Several make gestures around you; others cower. Even more bizarre—Princess Tamina begins to dance.

"What are you doing?" you demand.

"Diplomacy," she says through gritted teeth. Then she smiles at the group, and they all smile back at her. You, on the other hand, they don't seem so crazy about.

TURN TO PAGE 49

"And what about the Dagger," you press.

"Given to the girl whose goodness won man his reprieve," Tamina replies. "It's meant to be used in defense of the Sandglass. The blade is the only thing that can pierce the glass and remove the Sands of Time. The handle only holds one minute."

You look down at the weapon. "But if one were to place the Dagger in the Sandglass and press the jewel button at the same time . . ."

"Sand would flow through endlessly," Tamina confirms.

You stare at her. "And you could turn back time as far as you like."

Tamina puts her hand on your arm. "But it is forbidden!"

You nod as you put it all together. "When my father was a boy," you tell her, "Nizam saved his life while hunting. It's a story our father always repeated. It spoke of the strength of brotherhood."

You shake your head, wincing at the irony, now that you understand. "My uncle means to go back in time and undo what he did. *Not* save my father! Let him die! That would make him king. For a lifetime."

You and Tamina sit silently for a moment, considering everything. Then you realize how quiet it has become. "The storm's passed," you say.

TURN TO PAGE 117

You hit the jewel on the Dagger. Everything stops.

Then it begins to rewind. The vipers disappear underneath the sand and everyone goes back to sleep. You take note of the vipers' positions—including one you didn't notice before that is headed straight for Tamina.

You take a quick breath, steel your nerves, and release the jewel. The rewind stops, with a little bit of sand still left in the Dagger's handle.

The snakes instantly launch again, but now you're ready for them. You swing the Dagger and the burning log, ducking and spinning. You singe one viper, set another on fire, then slice a third in midair.

Only one more! You recall the viper's position and hurl the dagger—slicing the last snake in half as it leaps at Tamina.

The viper's head lands near Shiekh Amar. He kicks it away.

"Persian," Amar says in a shaking voice. "How—how did you do that?"

"Instincts," you reply.

Tamina looks at the Dagger, then smirks at you. But she keeps her mouth shut.

You notice dark silhouettes on a distant ridge. Sand dervishes move across the moonlit desert.

"We have to get out of here!" you cry. "Now!"

TURN TO PAGE 19

Sheikh Amar brings you into an underground salt mine. You seem to be standing at the edge of some kind of track. At one end, a large tattered Perisan rug hangs between two poles. Coming from behind it you hear screaming, shouting, chanting. You wonder what you've gotten yourself, and the princess, into. . . ?

A horrifying screech sends chills up your spine. The rug drops and . . .

They're off! About fifteen gangly birds run at full speed, wearing numbers on their chests and jockeys on their backs.

You turn and stare at Amar. "Ostrich racing?"

"What they lack in beauty, they make up for in fighting spirit," Amar says, grinning broadly. "And their races are easy to fix."

You watch the birds round the bend, your mouth open.

"Not what you were expecting, Persian?" Amar raises an eyebrow.

"I've heard the stories . . ." you admit.

"The bloodthirsty slaves that murdered their masters?" Amar intones dramatically. He bursts out laughing. "A great story. But alas, untrue."

"But the skeletons we saw," you sputter.

Amar shrugs. "Bought from a Gypsy in Bukhara. The real mine owner choked on a date pit."

You shake your head. Unbelievable!

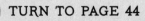

TURN TO PAGE 44

The guards bring you to the dungeon and shove you roughly into a cell. "Nizam was right," one of them says as he slams the heavy iron gate shut. "He predicted you'd sneak in through that doorway."

"You thought it was so secret," another one scoffs. "Don't you think as children you and your brothers were watched every moment? Whether you knew it or not?"

Moments later Nizam arrives. "Well, well, well," he says. "Were you looking for this?" He pulls the Dagger from his cloak.

You furiously lunge for him through the bars. "You killed your own family!" you shout. "How could you do that?"

"It was remarkably easy," Nizam tells you. He studies the Dagger. "All that struggle, all that death—over this. And in the end, I didn't even need to use it." He sheaths the dagger again. "All those who stood between me and the crown are gone."

"I'm still here," you remind him.

"The king's murderer will be executed soon enough," Nizam tells you. "The people will demand it." He eyes you, a sly smile crossing his face. "Though I think I'll keep you imprisoned a while. You've always been such a source of amusement to me."

He turns and strides away from your cell. You sink down onto the cold stone floor.

You vow you will avenge your family. Somehow. Someday. If you ever get out of this dungeon in . . .

THE END.

"We are victorious," Roham tells you. And only now do you notice the Persian soldiers herding bound groups of Alamutians out of the city.

"That's good news," you say. "So why do you look so stricken?"

"Your brothers," Roham says. He clamps his hands on your shoulders. "It is my burden to tell you they both died. They fought valiantly, but were cut down."

You swallow hard and then ask, "But the city is secured?"

"Yes," he assures you.

"Then I must get word to my father, King Sharaman. And to my uncle Nizam."

"I can bring you to Nizam," Roham says. "He's in the war-council tent, just outside the city walls. He's the one who sent me to find you."

You follow numbly behind. Perhaps Nizam will offer some solace. And with luck, your father will join you soon.

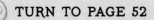**TURN TO PAGE 52**

"That stew sounds good," you tell her, keeping your voice level. "But I believe my horse would prefer hay. Is that something I can find here?"

Princess Tamina frowns, but makes no aggressive move. "I believe that can be arranged."

"I'll just wait here," you tell her. "My horse and I could use a drink." You grin. "And I could probably use a bath."

Now she smiles. It makes her all the more beautiful. "I'll be back."

Princess Tamina returns with a bowl of stew, and a stocky man carries over an armful of hay.

"Our village is humble," the man says, dropping the hay beside your horse. "But we will find you accommodations."

"That won't be necessary," you say. "I think we'll continue on our way."

"You seem troubled," Princess Tamina says. Her expression is concerned. "Is there something we can help you with?"

You shake your head. "This is something I need to do on my own," you tell her.

She nods as if she understands. "We all must seek our destinies, no matter how long it takes. It can be a lonely and challenging journey. But so rewarding. I know."

You have a feeling she does.

Mounting your horse, you once again head out into the unknown.

THE END

"Incredible," you say, figuring it out yourself. "Releasing the sand turns back time. And only the holder of the Dagger is aware of what's happened. He can go back, alter events, change time—and no one will know but him!"

You look up from the Dagger and stare at the princess. "How much can it unwind?"

She glares at you.

"Answer me, Princess!"

"You destroyed my city!" she shrieks at you.

"We had intelligence you were arming our enemies," you spit back.

"You had the lies of Persian spies," she says with a snarl.

Suddenly it all makes sense. Your grip tightens on the Dagger. "Our invasion wasn't about weapon forges," you say slowly. "It was about this Dagger."

"Clever prince," Tamina says bitterly.

You pace, all this information whirling around in your head. "After the battle, he asked for this Dagger as tribute. I didn't think anything of it. It was *Tus*. *He* gave me the gift that killed our father. *He* stands to be crowned king. With this Dagger, he'd be invincible." You gaze up at the sky, as if the stars hold answers. "Tus is behind it all. My *brother*."

TURN TO PAGE 99

"Douse your light," you whisper to Yusef. "We need to know what we're dealing with."

Yusef nods, and you both press your torches into the cool damp earth, killing the flames. A glow emanates from around the corner. You creep toward it as silently as possible.

You round the bend and gasp, stunned by what you see.

A crackling bonfire casts dancing shadows around a large chamber. The flames illuminate an astonishing treasury! Piles of gold coins, chests brimming with golden statues, candelabras, platters, jewels of every description. Unusual weapons are mixed in with glittering diadems and tiaras. The gems sparkle in the firelight, nearly blinding you.

Three rough-looking men sit on an overturned chest by the fire. One of them must have heard your sharp intake of breath. His eyes flick your way.

In an instant he's up and holding a scimitar.

TURN TO PAGE 60

You land with a thud in the courtyard below. You hold up the Dagger, panting.

"You did it!" Tamina cries. Then she gasps. "But you're hurt!"

She pulls one of the needles from your arm. In the heat of battle, you never even noticed it.

But the pain is only minimal. You have more important things to focus on. "Now to find Tus—make him understand the truth," you say.

TURN TO PAGE 79

"They'd want easy access to the forges and the weapons," you figure. "Let's take the tunnel running parallel to the street."

You hurry along the passageway. There's a sharp turn ahead. You step around the corner and . . . "Whoa!" you cry.

There's no ground beneath your feet! You drop your torch into the deep chasm below as you scramble to save yourself from falling.

It's no use. You claw, you scratch, you kick, but you still plummet deep down into the bowels of the earth.

THE END

Tamina's words have opened your eyes. You realize now that she and the Dagger are part of a larger destiny. Bigger than you and your need to clear your name.

"All right, Princess," you say. "We'll do it your way."

Relief floods her features. "Thank you." She holds out her hand for the Dagger.

"I don't think so." You slip it back into your belt. You know if she gets the Dagger she'll ditch you, leaving you alone in an unfamiliar landscape. And you need her to come back with you once this is all finished to help you prove your innocence.

You head north, and the terrain grows more treacherous. As you climb into the mountains a strange mist descends. You can barely see more than a few feet in front of you.

"Are we going the right way?" you ask.

"It's hard for me to find the landmarks in this mist," Tamina admits.

You stop for the night, hoping the mist will dissipate by morning.

As you had hoped, visibility has greatly improved by dawn the next day. But Tamina is worried. "I've never seen that village before," she says, pointing to the valley below. "We took a wrong turn somewhere."

"Maybe someone there can help us get back on track," you suggest. You mount Aksh and Tamina climbs up behind you. You slowly enter the village.

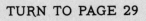 **TURN TO PAGE 29**

"You know me," you say to the crowd. "You know my love for my father. Why would I murder him? I would have nothing to gain!"

"Believe him!" Princess Tamina strides onto the stage. You can tell the crowd is taken with her beauty and her spirit. "Nizam orchestrated the siege against my city, a sacred site. All to take possession of this Dagger. He thought it would give him unlimited power!

"Dastan has behaved with honor," Princess Tamina continues. "I believe him innocent of any crimes of which he is accused." She whirls and glares at Nizam. "And accuse you of the most base treachery!"

Now a cry goes up: "Dastan! Dastan! Dastan!"

At first, you fear they are calling for your head. Then you spot Seso and Amar in the crowd, egging everyone on.

You take center stage. "Princess Tamina," you say, holding out the Dagger. "I believe this belongs to you."

She takes it from you, blinking back tears. You take her hand and turn so you're both facing the enormous crowd. "My family will not have died in vain!" you declare. "I make this vow to you that we shall forever live in peace from this day forward."

As the crowd cheers and shouts around you, you look at Tamina. "Your father would have been proud," she says. "This moment is what you were destined for."

You smile. For once, you think, the princess might be right!

THE END

You pull back the blanket to reveal dawn breaking over the desert. You help your horse get back up onto its hooves.

"Dastan," Tamina says, her voice urgent. "The sands contained within the Sandglass are volatile. Opening the Dagger while it's in the chamber breaks the seal. It could destroy the Sandglass. The Sands of Time would no longer be contained. And all of mankind would pay for Nizam's lust for power."

You look into her dark eyes. Is she finally telling you the truth? Or is this just another trick to get the Dagger back?

"The secret Guardian Temple outside Alamut is a sanctuary," she continues. "The Dagger must be delivered back to the safety of this sacred home. It's the only way to stop this Armageddon." She gazes up at you, her eyes filled with worry and pain. "That's the truth, Dastan. Give me back the Dagger so I can take it there."

You breathe in and out trying to decide. Then you slip the Dagger back into your belt. "I'm sorry, Princess. I can't do that."

Tamina stumbles back a step, her face flushed with fury and outrage.

Before she can light into you, you say, "I'm coming with you."

 TURN TO PAGE 78

It suddenly occurs to you that the village is awfully quiet. It seems . . . empty. Sheikh Amar goes to look around. You spot a hut with its door open. Tamina sees it as well and runs toward it.

You follow her and come across a horrifying sight. Four dead bodies are slumped against the house. They look to be priests.

Tamina gasps and drops to her knees. Clearly these people meant something to the princess. You put your hand on her shoulder.

Seso utters what sounds like a prayer, then says, "They have been dead a long time. Tortured first."

You study the bodies more carefully. "These wounds aren't from normal weapons."

"Hassansins?" Seso asks.

You nod grimly. "They were here. Nizam knows about this place."

Amar returns. "All dead," he reports. "The entire village."

TURN TO PAGE 93

That night, all but two guards are asleep. Although you're still bound, you try to think of some way to get the Dagger back and escape Sheikh Amar's grasp.

Seso has made himself a pillow by wrapping your sword and the dagger in his cloak. You're going to have to come up with something pretty amazing to get out of there alive—and with the princess and the dagger.

Wind blows through the camp. Aksh whinnies, disturbed by something.

Then you see why. A pit viper emerges from the sand in front of Seso. It rises up, forked tongue flickering. It coils to strike. You leap up and hurl a smoldering log. The snake goes flying into the darkness.

Seso stares at you. You can see that he knows you just saved his life. But there's no time for a thank you. Four furrows of sand weave through the camp.

"Give me the Dagger," you demand.

You hold out your bound hands. Seso hesitates, then his eyes grow wide when he sees the undulating furrows.

"If you want to live, give me the Dagger!" you insist.

Seso slashes the rope binding your hands and tosses you the Dagger. Just in time!

Three vipers burst from underneath the sand.

Do you use the Dagger to rewind time?
TURN TO PAGE 106.

But what if you use up all the sand? Do you battle them yourself? **TURN TO PAGE 100.**

120

The minute you step inside the city gates, you're swept up in hand-to-hand combat with an Alamutian sentry. He comes at you with his sword, and you meet it with yours, blocking it. You use your blade to push him back. He stumbles, but quickly recovers and charges at you again.

You spin around to gain momentum, then *clank!* Your sword hits his again. This time with so much power he's thrown off-balance.

Movement above you catches your attention. That's when you notice the archers up on the parapet.

Your split second of distraction gives your opponent his opening. He scrambles back to his feet.

Should you keep fighting him or should you run away, to try to find your men?

If you want to keep fighting, **GO TO PAGE 51.**

If you get out of there to try and find your men, **GO TO PAGE 84.**

You slowly turn to discover a group of men dressed in the dark clothes and turbans of the Hassansins. They have surrounded you, and their cold eyes peer from wind-blasted faces.

"You disappoint me," you say to them, squaring your shoulders and tightening the grip on your sword. Princess Tamina stares at you. You ignore her and take a step toward them.

"I came here to train with the deadliest of fighters. Yet we were able to infiltrate your compound. We were here for some time before your *pets*"—you tip your head toward the dead vipers—"came to greet us."

One of the men comes forward. "Who sent you to us?" he demands.

You smirk. "You don't recognize me?" you ask. "I was sent by the very one who brought you back together. Who created this training camp." You hope this ruse will get you the information you need.

The man raises an eyebrow and then nods. "Of course. You are Dastan. But I thought your uncle Nizam had kept our existence a secret from your family."

You force yourself not to betray your shock at his words. "Uncle Nizam isn't going to be pleased if I tell him I caught you all unawares."

You see his jaw clench and his hand go to his weapon. "I will be happy to tell him you have been training hard and training well," you add.

"Who is the woman?" another man asks. "Why would Nizam want you to bring a woman among us?"

Why indeed?

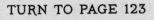 **TURN TO PAGE 123**

You cannot take your eyes off the bundle. Odd. A strange light seems to illuminate the fabric from within.

Glancing around to make sure no attackers lie in wait, you drop into a crouch and open the bundle. Inside is a beautiful ceremonial dagger. It looks ancient and somehow . . . *otherwordly*. An intricate pattern decorates the jagged blade. The glass handle is filled with white sand so unnaturally bright it seems to glow. You raise the Dagger to the light and watch the sands shift.

You feel frozen in time, as if you were hypnotized by the beauty of the object, the trickling grains of sand.

A cry of victory snaps you out of your reverie. The Persian army has taken the city!

You slip the Dagger into your belt and head out to find your brothers.

Join in the victory and GO TO PAGE 6.

"She is to be trained as well," you say. "A woman can sometimes accomplish things a man cannot."

The Hassansin looks skeptical, but he doesn't ask any more questions.

"May we have a tour?" you ask. You want to get a lay of the land. You're going to need to get out of there quickly—get word to your brothers about Nizam's betrayal.

"I'd like to see the weapons," Princess Tamina says, her voice cold and haughty. "I'm trained in many already. I'd like to try something new."

"Trainees don't give orders," the Hassansin growls. He turns to you. "I'd like to see *your* weapons. That Dagger is most unusual."

Something glints in the sunlight—all of the men have drawn weapons.

"In fact, that Dagger looks exactly like the one Nizam has charged us to find," he adds.

They're on to you!

You know they'll chase you and not the princess, since they're after the Dagger. You spin around and bang into her—and secretly slip it into her hands. "Run!" you cry. She takes off—and you race in the opposite direction.

As you suspected, they're all on your trail. You'll never beat them; you won't outrun them, you can't outfight them.

But at least the princess will get the Dagger to safety.

THE END

You make your way into the cave, the sound of fighting growing fainter. Finally you come to a deep natural pool. Tamina stands in the water in front of a rock altar. She lifts the Dagger, about to plunge it into the sacred stone.

Vwhip! A whip wraps around her wrist, yanking her backward. The Dagger goes flying!

You pull out a sword—just in time. You block another whip blade before it can cut Tamina in half.

You turn, gripping your sword, ready to face the assailant—a Hassansin. You need to get him away from Tamina and the sacred stone.

You somersault under more whip blades, then leap up and retreat back outside. You leap onto the roof of a farmhouse. The Hassansin follows you, his whips hissing as they flick and curl.

You raise your sword and catch one of the whips. It wraps around your blade and you tug hard, leaning out with all your weight. The other whip blade slashes at you, slicing open your shirt. You twist, turn, and sever the blades from the rest of the whips.

But the Hassansin doesn't give up. He pulls out a sword and charges.

TURN TO PAGE 95

"I'm not," you protest. "And that's what I'm here to prove."

Bis's sister backs away from you and sits. You kneel in front of her and take her hands in yours. "Bis died protecting me," you say gently. "He knew I would never harm my father. Your brother was a brave man. And my good friend."

"Bis loved you like a brother." She gazes at you with tear-filled eyes. "I never believed the talk," she assures you. "What do you need? How can I help?"

"I need all the news about Nizam," you tell her. "And a place to stay for the night."

The next morning, wearing Bis's clothes and carrying several of his weapons, you head for the palace courtyard. Bis's sister has told you Nizam is to be crowned king today.

Not if you have anything to say about it, you think.

Your fists clench as you take in the scene. There is a great deal of security, you note. Nizam stands on a platform surrounded by bodyguards, and archers are positioned on rooftops. You sneak through the crowd, keeping your head down until you reach the edge of the platform.

The moment arrives. The regent carries the crown to Nizam as he puts on the ceremonial robes. This is your last chance to stop it.

You leap up onto the platform. "Stop!" you cry. "You are giving the empire to the king's *true* murderer!"

TURN TO PAGE 88

"I will talk to Father," you tell Nizam. "It's important he know that Tus and Garsiv did not die in vain. That will only happen if we find those forges and put an end to the Alamutians' dealings with our enemies."

"Good," Nizam says. "Let me know what happens."

You steel yourself to face your father. You battle the pain you feel—both at the loss of your brothers, but also at the idea that despite everything, your father never truly cared for you the way he did for them. But you have a mission to accomplish, and emotions won't help you.

You arrive at the chambers where your father is staying. A guard bars your entrance.

"He's not seeing anyone," the guard tells you.

"He'll see me," you insist.

"He was very clear," the guard says. "You are one of the people he *specifically* does not want to see."

Your heart sinks. This is what you were afraid of. Nizam was right. Your father has turned against you.

TURN TO PAGE 128

There's no way that you trust her. "Forget it, Princess."

You race out of the courtyard. She's following you, so you take every twist and turn and finally you lose her.

But you have also lost yourself!

You have no idea where you are—this is a strange city and you just ran wherever your feet took you. You slow to a walk and step out of an alley.

And find yourself in the courtyard of the palace! You ran right back to where you started!

"The murderer!" a voice calls out. "Get him!"

A volley of arrows streaks through the night sky from all directions. A searing pain radiates through your body. Your eyes flutter and you realize this is . . .

THE END.

In despair, you pack a few meager provisions and head out to the stables. You see no point in staying. If you were not welcomed by your father, then you are not welcome in the kingdom. You have no future here.

You ride north. You're not sure why, other than that it is away from Nasaf, your home. Your former home, you remind yourself.

For days you ride up into the mountains, never seeing a single other soul. The desolate landscape matches your mood. If only you had kept your brothers from invading. They would still be alive, and you would still be in your father's favor.

But would you really? According to Nizam, Sharaman never saw you as a real son. So even if you had changed the events, it wouldn't have made one bit of difference. You would still be the outsider.

How could I have not seen it? you wonder as you lead your horse along a heavily wooded trail. King Sharaman always made you feel we were close, that your bond was just as strong as his bonds with Tus and Garsiv.

You emerge from the trees and look down upon a tiny village in the valley below. Perhaps they will allow you to spend the night there, water your horse, and add to your provisions.

TURN TO PAGE 73

You grab the torch. You don't want to risk your neck by running in the dark.

You round several more corners, and by the time you take the fourth or fifth forked passage you're pretty sure you've lost Ogav and his pals. You slow down.

You need to take a break. And you've got to come up with a way out of here. Otherwise you may be doomed to spend the rest of your life underground!

You lean against a wall—and tumble backward! Somehow you tripped a secret doorway.

Shaking your head, you find yourself in a giant chamber filled with sand. Your jaw drops as you stare at a towering structure. It looks like an enormous hourglass.

You step toward it and trip, sending the torch flying. It hits the glass and you hear a sharp ping! Luckily it just created the tiniest of nicks.

No one will notice that, you figure. Phew! A trickle of sand drains out of the minuscule hole. No big deal.

Then images suddenly begin to whirl around you. You watch in astonishment as you see yourself enter the chamber! It's as if time is rewinding in front of your very eyes!

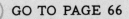 **GO TO PAGE 66**

Nizam's cold lust for power enrages you. You scream and lunge at him, swinging your sword. Nizam lifts the Dagger to block and you knock it out of his hands. Nizam cowers, waiting for you to deal a deathblow.

"I trusted you," you tell him.

You stand over your uncle, struggling to bring yourself to kill him. Suddenly he reaches into his cloak and pulls out a short-blade knife. He slashes you across your gut. You drop to your knees.

"Dastan!" Tamina cries from her hiding place.

Nizam rushes to recover the Dagger. "I never understood why my brother brought trash into his palace," he says, crossing to the Sandglass. "Enjoy the gutter, Dastan. It's where you'll stay under my reign."

He raises the Dagger, ready to pierce the Sandglass and rewind time to the moment when he saved his brother. Only this time, he won't.

But when he breaks the seal, he will bring down utter distruction.

Another tremor, and cracks appear in the floor. Nizam stumbles as the ground shakes.

"Don't use the Dagger," you plead. "It will unleash—"

"Unleash what?" Nizam cuts you off. "God's wrath? Hell itself? Better to rule in hell than grovel upon the face of this cursed earth!"

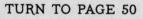

TURN TO PAGE 50

"Let it go!" you shout at Nizam.

"Never! This is my time now!" he roars back at you.

Sand pours out of the Dagger as ghostly images of you and Nizam float backward through the actions you just performed. You see yourself somersault in reverse, landing on the column. You see Tamina clinging to the edge of the chasm. Then you watch her fall *up* and back onto the ground, where she totters.

You could go to her and keep her from ever falling in. But that would mean you'd have to let go of the Dagger. Is your destiny to save Tamina or the Dagger?

If you rush to Tamina,
TURN TO PAGE 132.

If you cling to the Dagger, **TURN TO PAGE 133.**

Y ou can't lose Tamina. You leap from the Sandglass platform to grab her. Your sudden movement jerks the Dagger out of Nizam's grip—and out of the Sandglass!

You topple backward and manage to steady yourself beside Tamina just at the edge of the chasm. The Dagger skitters to a stop just a few inches from you and the sand stops flowing. You bend to grab the Dagger.

"NO!" Nizam lunges for it. You swiftly move out of his path, and his momentum carries him right into the abyss. He falls, screaming the whole way down.

You take a deep breath. It's over. You pick up the Dagger and hold it out to Tamina.

"I believe this is yours," you say.

She takes it, her eyes full of tears. "You did it," she whispers.

"*We* did it," you say. "And now the world can be safe again. All is as it should be. We have each met the challenge of our destinies."

THE END

If you don't stop Nizam and the flow of sand out of the Sandglass, it won't matter if you save Tamina! The Sandglass will shatter—and all of humanity may perish!

Time continues to stream backward as you struggle to make Nizam release the dagger. The Sandglass begins to creak angrily as if it's about to shatter!

You let out a powerful, guttural bellow as you summon the strength to shove Nizam away from you. He stumbles and you yank the Dagger from the Sandglass.

Whoosh!

The rewind stops, and the hole where the Dagger pierced the glass miraculously closes up. You feel dizzy and faint. . . . You shut your eyes for just a moment.

TURN TO PAGE 134

You open your eyes to see a man lying before you in an alleyway. You clutch an embroidered cloth. You open the cloth and discover the Dagger inside.

You've gone back to when you fought with Princess Tamina's guard, who was trying to sneak the Dagger out of the city to safety. To where this adventure all began.

You clutch the Dagger. This time, though, things will be different. You will make different choices. Change the course of events.

This time you will be all that your father hoped you would be—not simply a good man, but a great one. And your father will live to see it happen. You now know the power of the Dagger and the secrets of Alamut. Perhaps Princess Tamina was right after all— that you had a destiny, and it was to bring you back to this moment when you could make things right.

THE END

Want the adventure to continue?
Find out what journeys Dastan goes on in:

It's YOUR Call
with more than 20 possible endings

Disney **PRINCE OF PERSIA**
THE SANDS OF TIME

THE GUARDIAN'S PATH

Written by Carla Jablonski
Based on the screenplay written by Doug Miro & Carlo Bernard
From a screen story by Jordan Mechner and Boaz Yakin
Executive Producers Mike Stenson, Chad Oman, John August, Jordan Mechner,
Patrick McCormick, Eric McLeod
Produced by Jerry Bruckheimer
Directed by Mike Newell

TURN THE PAGE FOR A SNEAK PEEK!

Prologue

You were born with a sacred duty, a destiny. Like your ancestors, you have a responsibility so great there have been times you wondered if the burden was too much to bear. For you, Princess Tamina, are charged with protecting the very fabric of time—as a Guardian. You have been given the task of keeping the secrets of the Sandglass of Time safe and of protecting its mystical Dagger.

However, you fear now that all your beliefs are about to be tested. The barbaric Persians are outside the gates of your holy city of Alamut, putting the Dagger in danger. You hope you will be able to rise to this moment and live up to your destiny.

You stand in your chamber as your attendants paint you with sacred henna tattoos.

"Princess Tamina," a voice says.

You turn to see the Regent of Alamut, bearded and bent with age, standing in the doorway.

"Enter," you say. The Regent steps into your lush chamber. You don't like the serious expression on his face; it bodes trouble.

"The Persian army, my princess," he says. "It has not moved on. I fear—"

You cut him off. "Show me," you say.

TURN TO PAGE 2

You walk briskly outside and out along the ramparts of Alamut's walls. The Regent and your bodyguards hurry to keep up. The stars glitter in the dark sky, but clouds cover the moon, making even these well-known walkways seem ominous.

Now you see other flickering lights—below you, on the ground. Fires from the Persian camp. They are preparing for an attack, you are certain.

"My princess," the Regent calls, "perhaps it would be safer if you didn't stand so close to the edge."

You clutch the rough stone, drumming your fingers. Their numbers are great; but your convictions are greater.

"Gather council," you tell the Regent. "Tell them I sit in the High Temple. I must pray." You turn from the rampart and head up a winding staircase.

The Regent follows behind you, confused. "The High Temple? Alamut hasn't been breached in a thousand years." He does not say it aloud but you know his concern—that the Persians will take the city and discover its secrets.

"Everything changes in time," you say, without breaking stride. "We should know this best of all."

TURN TO PAGE 3

The ornate High Temple sits above the city, nestled among the clouds. You spend the night in prayer with your retinue, seeking the strength and wisdom you'll need to face what's to come.

At dawn, an Alamutian soldier bursts into your sanctuary. "Persians have breached the eastern gates!" he cries.

All eyes turn to you. "Collapse the passages to the chamber," you order. "Go now, all of you." They file out of the temple, casting worried glances at you. Only a tall, elegant warrior stays behind. This is your trusted advisor, Asoka.

"Above all else," you say, repeating the words you've heard all your life, "it must be saved. Yes, Asoka?"

"Yes, Princess," Asoka says.

You kneel before an ornate column. You touch your forehead to the floor and stretch out your arms. You whisper the ancient words. There is a soft rumble, and a radiant light pours out of the column as it swings open.

You stand and step inside the revealed tabernacle. You take a glowing dagger from its resting place and wrap it in an embroidered cloth. It is more powerful than anyone might imagine.

The Dagger *must* be kept safe.

Should you give it to Asoka to take out of the city or should you do it yourself?

If you give it to Asoka to take to the Guardian Temple in the North, TURN TO PAGE 10.

If you believe you should take it yourself,
TURN TO PAGE 85.